D1474511

I Carry A Hammer In My Pocket
For Occasions Such As These

I Carry A Hammer In My Pocket For Occasions Such As These

❖ ❖ ❖

stories by
ANTHONY TOGNAZZINI

AMERICAN READER SERIES, NO. 8

BOA EDITIONS, LTD. ❖❖❖ ROCHESTER, NY ❖❖❖ 2007

First Edition
07 08 09 10   7 6 5 4 3 2 1

Publications by BOA Editions, Ltd.—a not-for-profit corporation under section 501
(c) (3) of the United States Internal Revenue Code—are made possible with the
assistance of grants from the Literature Program of the New York State Council
on the Arts; the Literature Program of the National Endowment for the Arts; the
County of Monroe, NY; the Lannan Foundation for support of the Lannan Transla-
tions Selection Series; the Sonia Raiziss Giop Charitable Foundation; the Mary S.
Mulligan Charitable Trust; the Rochester Area Community Foundation; the Arts
& Cultural Council for Greater Rochester; the Steeple-Jack Fund; the Elizabeth F.
Cheney Foundation; Eastman Kodak Company; the Chesonis Family Foundation;
the Ames-Amzalak Memorial Trust in memory of Henry Ames, Semon Amzalak
and Dan Amzalak; and contributions from many individuals nationwide.

See Colophon on page 144 for special individual acknowledgments.

Cover Design: Steve Smock, Prime 8 Media
Cover Art: Erica Harris
Interior Design and Composition: Richard Foerster
Manufacturing: McNaughton & Gunn, Lithographers
BOA Logo: Mirko

Library of Congress Cataloging-in-Publication Data

Tognazzini, Anthony.
  I carry a hammer in my pocket for occasions such as these / Anthony Tognazzini. — 1st ed.
      p. cm. — (American reader series ; no. 8)
    ISBN 978-1-929918-90-4 (pbk. : alk. paper)
    I. Title.

PS3620.O3255I3 2006
811'.6—dc22

                                                    2006030020

NATIONAL
ENDOWMENT
FOR THE ARTS

BOA Editions, Ltd.
Nora A. Jones, Executive Director/Publisher
Thom Ward, Editor/Production
Peter Conners, Editor/Marketing
Glenn William, BOA Board Chair
A. Poulin, Jr., President & Founder (1938–1996)
260 East Avenue, Rochester, NY 14604
www.boaeditions.org

State of the Arts

NYSCA

Table of Contents

Ever Since This Morning

Second Thoughts

The Vow of I Never Want to Open My Eyes

The Unfortunate Poker Game

Gift Exchange

❖ ❖ ❖

I Carry A Hammer In My Pocket

For Occasions Such As These

❖ ❖ ❖

Ever Since
This Morning

A Primer

We were drinking coffee when the naked man arrived. His bare ass flashed as he ran down the hall. A minute later he came back with a large can of paint. Naturally, we worried. We chewed our lower lips. This naked man had a metal box, which he set on the floor and opened. He picked out the thickest bristled brush, dipped it in the paint can, and began to paint his torso. "Hey now," we said. Baby blue drops spattered all over as the naked man worked in vertical strokes from neck to midriff, over his shoulders and under his underarms. "There," he said when he finished. "The shirt." The naked man went down the hall again, his butt wobbling beneath blue shirt flaps. He came back with a can of green paint. With one of the thinner brushes he made straight lines along his legs. "The pants!" he cried. We tried to keep from yelling when the naked man ran out again. He returned with some smaller paint cans. With regular acrylic he brushed on brown shoes; he used a needlepoint brush to create tan laces, threading them into painted-on eyelets. He dunked a brush in screaming red, then slathered on a jacket. He daubed on a hat, scarf, gloves, and a long, woolen overcoat which he painted up button by button. Beneath the black fabric, his colors were still there, but hidden, and beating like a heart. A finished picture, the naked man stood in the doorway and waved. We waved back as he vanished in the landscape.

Double Trouble

I came home and discovered that my house had been turned into a museum. I'd expected something else—a marching band, maybe, or a little pile of cinders, not an usher in a plush coat seated by my mailbox.

"Eight bucks," he said, and gave me a burgundy pennant.

I re-checked the address: It was mine. I felt my hands, my hips, the bones in my nose: They were mine.

Inside, a crowd milled through the rooms, holding brochures. They stroked their chins in contemplation. They were eyebrow-raised, gum-chewing sorts. Five or six people had crowded in the shower, fondling the soap and fixtures. A translator spoke to a Japanese family who'd bottlenecked the hall.

I understood their curiosity. I was curious too.

In the kitchen, at the sink, others edged in to see my breakfast dishes: a white plate streaked with caked egg yolk, a dot-connecting treasure trail of toast crumbs. "Hmm," said a man with a camera, and clicked.

A tour group passed through my bedroom. Casually, like two hands detaching at the end of a handshake, I slipped out of myself to join them.

Around us, red-haired wives brandished camcorders. "This is where he slept," we marveled. My comb, toothbrush, and a pair of white socks were held up for examination:

"Documents of the vanished man," we said.

Even with the newly installed ventilation system, the air in our lungs felt thin and official. We moved past the window and stared at the chair on the picturesque porch, thinking how his

14

body must have rested. Nearby, in a large display case, photographs and notebooks were pinned like butterflies—testament to the difference between life and its distance.

Someone said, "Wow."

We wondered—each of us, in the rooms of our viewing—if this is what death must be like.

And now we know it is.

Many Fine Marriages Begin at Friends' Parties

Because she looked like an ex-girlfriend of mine, I thought she might be attracted to me too. "Kelly?" I said from the chips, and reached to touch her shoulder.

She turned around, and looked as if she were studying a puzzle, or hard at a task that required attention, like threading a needle, or soldering wires on a small transistor radio.

I said, "Oh, sorry. I thought you were someone else. In profile you look exactly like my old girlfriend. Your nose has a big monstrous bump in the middle, same as her. It's a great bump, though. It looks like an incredibly sexy knuckle. Have you tried this dip? Isn't it funny how we feel connected with people who remind us of someone we know? I mean, I felt compelled to talk to you, like something is between us, even though we're total strangers. And you're so beautiful, I thought we might go out to the gazebo and tell each other some secrets."

Her eyes could have liquefied a rock. For a second I thought she might slap me. Then she said, "In no other instance could the word 'lost' mean more. What we think we own, we don't. Our thoughts are insubstantial, our limbs thin as sticks, our words rip apart in the wind, and the heart—it aches and aches."

I looked at her, amazed. "Marry me," I whispered. She gave a little giggle and said, "The soul can't know its own shadow, and besides, you've got guacamole on your glasses."

In Love With Nowhere To Go

When I came to I discovered the furniture had been removed from the room. Gone the bed frame, the nightstand, and the fire truck lamp. The walls were bright white. My face registered no surprise.

I stepped from the bedroom as if to meet an opponent, and the bareness of the living room leapt at me. A ring of dust spread where the La-Z-Boy had been. I kicked off my one remaining slipper.

"Well," I said.

"For God's sake," I said.

I went into the kitchen and found the furniture stacked up at crazed angles. Sofa cushions in the sink, La-Z-boy on the stove. I climbed over cabinets to reach the refrigerator, found a glass of tomato juice, and poured it down my throat thick and pulpy. I put the dirty glass in a desk drawer. My fish-white feet were bare.

When I tried to say "Good morning," my lips stuck together.

What had happened the night before I couldn't remember. The only thing I heard was the sound of Jane's voice-- which, in memory, was soft and repetitious.

I remembered that I was in love. I ran out to my car, a 1957 Nash Rambler with peeling paint and no hubcaps. I got behind the wheel and drove eighty miles an hour to a shopping mall downtown. In the parking lot of the mall I drove forty in circles, round and around, reading a biography of Jane and me. I propped the book on the dashboard and steered with my knees. My bare feet punched the clutch and accelerator. The biography was interesting but was written in a dry, academic style, so I threw it out the window. I turned on the radio. It was Jane's voice. I said, "All right."

Tires swirled rubber across gray, steaming asphalt. I was in love with nowhere to go. The mall was a long brown block I was speeding past.

Realizing I was thirsty, I went to a drive-thru liquor store called Stop and Sop. The microphone at the drive-thru was disguised as a plastic beer bottle.

"Hello," I said.

"Murf, murf," said the lady.

I told her she'd better articulate herself or else.

She said, "From this blanket of ashes, our Life, springs not one but a thousand dancing angels, their hearts dappled flags of moonlight, their wings slim and silvery."

So I said, "From infancy to the grave we march a ragged line, huddling under our broken cloaks—attenuating our treasure, our warm wilting hope, our bright final flower."

I drove up to the window, revving the engine. The lady leaned out in her red and white uniform.

"People are precious as prizes," she said.

I told her that was only alliteration.

She gave me five bottles of whiskey and I peeled out of the parking lot, swerving the tires everywhichway to leave good-looking skid marks.

On the freeway I did eighty. I rolled down the windows and threw out the cigarette lighter and the lid to the glove compartment. I ripped out the rearview mirror. When I polished off two of the bottles, my driving improved. I said, "Oh yeah."

I got home the next morning and remembered the furniture. The white walls whirled. My stomach jumped like an angry, barking dog and I spun, throwing up in every direction. When I finished, I regarded the abstract, brown-red splashes on the tile. I thought, Pollock.

Brushing my teeth, I began to grow tired. The mirror showed a face heavy with its immense, gruesome smile and I remembered

I'd been in my pajamas all night and day. I noticed I'd dribbled some toothpaste on the collar.

"Nobody knows," I sang to myself.

I went into the kitchen, singing, and threw my car keys on the drain board. I climbed onto the couch, which was balanced on the counter, the cutting boards and spice jars. I squirmed around trying to get comfortable. The shades were up and sun streamed through the window and pounded my face. I felt my brain moving at eighty miles an hour; I was alone in my day-old pajamas and my songs were the only thing I knew. I sang myself to sleep with a knife-like voice.

Eavesdropping at the Van Gogh Museum

I think they've got those sunflowers here.   Let's meet by the entrance at six.   He was going to be a clergyman, you know. Excuse me.   This olive grove is cooler.   Do the words 'sincere human feeling' mean anything to you?   It's Prussian blue.   The sky looks like the inside of a down comforter.   When you stand close to this one it looks like nothing at all.   Step back, doofus. The series represents different selves.   They got some irises over here that are just gonna knock you out.   Do you mind?   The almond trees are stuttering.   His room at Arles looks comfortable enough, sure, but just imagine, no T.V.   Pardon me.   I read his mother had a stillborn a year before him and the baby was going to be named Vincent.   He was the ghost of someone else.   Get closer.   I mean... if you move your head this way, it's just... Oh, I don't know, I can't explain it.   An egg-yolk viewed through an emerald.   My Motrin's in my suitcase, which is at the hotel. He did what he couldn't do to learn how to do it.   That's talent. Look at this one and tell me that's not talent!   The turquoise of a dog's fever.   The sky's alive.   It was the world's nature versus his, he knew he'd lose: that's why he was like that.   Todd, will you please *shut up*!   How wrong fundamentally is the man who does not realize he's but an atom?   My feet.   I'm sorry.   What happened to his ear, eventually?—that's what I want to know.   He never considered a painting finished.   The sky looks like a piece of melted plastic.   Can we go now?   Yes.   The rage of life's beauty trying to get out of him.   The gift shop's still open.   That's true.   Everything seems to be vibrating.   That's absolutely true.

Macho Outing

My friend Ed came over with his competitive personality, oversized lumberjack shirt, and cottage cheese complexion. He knocked on the door with the force of a storm, hollering, "Hey." From the screen I saw him shadowboxing on the lawn, smashing my gladiolas.

"Wanna do a little sparring?" he asked with a jab. "I got an extra pair of gloves in the garage."

Ed pantomimed an uppercut, smiled, wagged his eyebrows.

I said, "I don't think I feel up to any gratuitous displays of brute masculinity right now. How about something else?"

Ed shrugged. "Old-fashioned arm-wrestling match?"

I sat down on the front step, took a deep breath. "Look," I said, "Maybe we could go somewhere. You know, do something?"

Ed did not agree, exactly.

I said, "Let's go ice skating."

We drove down to the Mission Valley Mall and walked side by side through the great glass doors into the architecturally spacious area where they have a triple-tiered food court and a video game arcade. Ed and I played doubles on Space Invaders, then rented some skates and went around the rink a couple times. Tinny Christmas music blared overhead as we wobbled by eight-year-old girls in white outfits. Ed looked funny among them, slishing tentatively over the ice with his little scissor steps.

"I've never done this before," he said, and just at that moment his legs shot out from under him and in a great windmilling of arms he fell back, smack on his ass. I looked at him: full bulk splayed in the middle of the rink, red shirt white with snowy powder, expression like shame but distinct from it.

"That's obvious," I said, and we both laughed.

Later, we got some raspberry sherbet from Haskin's, and ate it with gusto at a cramped plastic table. We watched the other skaters dip and pirouette. "That was really fun," Ed kept saying, over and over. The sherbet made his mouth look blood-filled. I could tell he was in terrible pain. I looked on as he ground his teeth, clutching the cone in his fist like a prize.

The Day We Were Set Free

I had the 4th off from work, and nothing to do, so I walked outside to water the lawn. It looked as if it were about to rain though, so I figured *What's the point?* and went back in the house. But the phone was ringing off the hook—bill collectors, wrong numbers—and it was working my nerves, so I stepped onto the front porch and stood there awhile in my flip-flops.

I gazed at the sky. The sun was smashing up the dark clouds and breaking through clear and beautiful. A gorgeous Independence Day. I wished I had a flag to fly, or some fireworks to send off in a peal of red and purple. I wanted to celebrate the liberation of our great nation.

Instead, some Hare Krishnas came dancing up the carport. Their bald heads were sweaty, and slow, steady motion made their silky robes billow.

"I'm not interested," I said.

They told me they weren't out to proselytize, but were taking up a collection to have an air conditioner installed in their meditation center.

"It's unbelievably hot in there," the Krishnas explained. "Have a heart." I had no money, but went down to the basement to retrieve an old fan. The antique thing was in poor condition—blades rust-mottled, wirework covered with cobwebs—but when I brought it outside and watched their reactions, each Krishna face glowed as though connected to an outlet.

"Eternity will welcome you and the blue lotus will be your bed," they said.

I must have blushed.

All the Krishnas smiled with teeth and drifted in their robes up the street with my fan.

Westminster March

Scott Terreto is second chair clarinet in the school band and I am first chair clarinet and that is why he hates me, I guess—saying, when he whips his Levi's jacket off the floor after practice, in a voice so loud that everyone can hear, "You're gonna get it, Tory Haimen," even though Scott's parents have more money than mine and can go to Simmond's music shop and buy him an expensive clarinet and a steady supply of new reeds and my parents had to get my clarinet at the second hand store, he is still full of bitterness because he is not as good as I am and inferiority rankles, I guess, and for him it's like a constant battering of the ego with the humility stick, I guess, and that's why he glares poison arrows across the band room with his green eyes which are actually the color of old celery, contrasting so cruelly with his straw-blonde hair and screaming red acne that one is forced to admit the plain, sad truth that Scott Terreto is *not cute*, and no girls, least of all Lisa Meyer, whose heavily-shampooed hair drapes the first chair in the flute section, will go out with him.

Least of all Lisa Meyer whose light lips pucker over the oblong hole of her flute and whose sweet breath condenses there on the chrome, whose eyes stray shyly in my direction when we're playing "Westminster March" and I wink over the music stand and she tries not to giggle because she knows we're going to meet behind Pizza Hut after practice to make out. I shoot a quick glance beside me and see that Scott has seen the whole subtle exchange and my glance makes him so mad he accidentally skips a cadenza and says *Shit!* out loud and the band teacher, Mr. Dougherty, taps his little baton for us to stop and tells Scott, in front of everyone, that he should try to have a better attitude, that he's never going to have a crack at first chair if he doesn't make a more positive effort, and Scott's acned face turns even redder, but I try not to feel too bad because, I reason philosophically, that's just life in eighth grade, you know?

But I do feel bad for him anyway when all the girls in the flute section giggle and point at him and I can see he's really embarrassed and his hand goes self-consciously to the bandage on his arm where he's getting the long, painful series of rabies shots, which is something I know about because I was kind of responsible for Scott getting rabies in the first place because of that afternoon when Lisa and I were making out in the parking lot behind Pizza Hut and we caught Scott spying on us from behind the dumpster and when I shouted his name and started to run toward him he threw a tennis ball at me and yelled, "Tory Haimen, you suck!" then took off running before I could get to him, but he'd accidentally left his books there (his History book and his Introduction to Algebra book) and I was so p.o.ed I threw them in the dumpster. Lisa said that wasn't very nice but laughed anyway and we were surprised the next day when Scott wasn't at band practice and the teacher told us that Scott had to go to the hospital to begin a series of excruciating injections to counteract the rabies virus he might have contracted from a rat bite he got while playing around in a dumpster.

And the day *after* there was a school-wide bulletin announced in every class which warned us kids against playing in dumpsters because we might get bitten by rats and the bulletin mentioned Scott Terreto by name and I guess that's when everyone started calling him Rabie-Face, which I had to admit was not nice but pretty funny, and right now, when the whole class is laughing at him for saying *Shit!* out loud and being yelled at by the teacher, one of the trumpet players says, "Good goin' Rabie-Face" and Scott gets so mad that he throws down his new, expensive clarinet and storms out of the band room, pushing over my music stand as he blows by me hoping, I assume, that I'll feel threatened, but I don't because Lisa looks over at me, eyes brimming with tenderness and admiration and I feel strong in love, knowing that one day we'll be married and have a nice apartment of our own where she'll play flute in the kitchen and I'll get constantly to kiss her mouth which is soft as ice cream and sweeter.

The Metaphysics of Orange Juice

Eight hours later you're up in the same body, stumbling from the room, grazing a knee on the nightstand. In the kitchen your hand finds the refrigerator, brings back a glass of juice. Your throat works thirstily. When you're done, the o.j.'s in you and every item in sight—the dish drainer, the fruit bowl—goes slowly orange. The sweet running sun behind the blinds is orange. The twenty minutes left to get to work is orange. In your mind's eye, which is orange, you see yourself at a desk all day, and though you're aware it's bad form to go unenchanted so long, the years pass quickly, and always you are like a dog running toward the edge of a field where your rubber doggie bone, also orange, is hidden, but the field keeps receding and you are more and more tired, more and more confused, but *running*. You're in front of a refrigerator. You know this white door—with its jostling pickle and jam jars—is like any door: a sense of cold shock behind a familiar façade, and on the other side of that, relief. The rest of your day will squeeze by inconspicuous. Driving to work in the Cabriolet. The mailman will bring the same letters. But just look at yourself: hands like round hammers, eyes orange portals set to click and deliquesce. Now look at the clock. It's time to get dressed. At the closet you pull on a pair of fresh socks, scramble into pants. Slowly you put on an orange shirt backwards, feeling more awake than you ever thought possible.

The Difference

Although I was never an early riser, my father always counseled me to rise with the sun.

"Early bird gets the worm!" he told me.

"Sure," I said, "but the worm who sleeps late, lives."

Teresa's Second Dream

This year, in a brightly lit living room, Teresa will stand up from the couch, smooth her silk pleated skirt, fluff hair with hands, check long dangling earrings, purse lips to a lipsticked pucker, and cross to the door. Painted nails and a light summer blouse become her. She will have gotten up to answer the doorbell. Shrill ring of the doorbell in the brightly lit living room. Never, not once in her nineteen years of life, has Teresa been with a man. She'll note the deep pillows on the divan. She'll eye the brown shag carpet, considering. She'll open the door. It's a man. The man comes in and kisses her on the cheek in a socially acceptable way. They marry. They live together for many years, the chandelier in the living room elegantly tinkling, the toaster most modern. There will be a Mitsubishi in the two-car garage and a child named Maximilian whose grades in arithmetic are not up to par. Midwestern winters will be cold, mufflers and gloves will be required at all times. Occasionally they will turn on the television.

They will see a show about a secret agent named Jack Yammer who can change himself into any manufactured metal at will. In this episode Jack Yammer is being chased by a gang of pimps through a downtown shopping district and turns himself into a ball of aluminum foil. They will turn the television off. The man and Teresa, Teresa and the man. White wine on the couch and desultory conversation will be the tenor of their evenings, after Max has been put to bed. One night they'll be discussing first memories. The husband will tell Teresa the story of when he was four and playing with his mother on the living room carpet. Carried away by the sense of play, he'd reached up, grabbed hold of his mother's shiny earrings, and yanked them through her lobes. Blood, screams, handfuls of cotton.

"That's horrible," Teresa will say.

Suddenly, without warning, the man will reach up and pull the earrings out of Teresa's ears. Blood, screams, handfuls of cotton in the brightly lit living room. Teresa will think how we can never really know that which we think we know. She'll call the police, who'll come and cart the husband away: raving, face tear-streaked, hands still clutching the gleaming earrings.

Teresa will decide to take a short walk to think about the nature of things. The nature of things, by and large, is not so good, she thinks, fingering her shredded lobes.

She'll decide to move to Mexico with Max and get a job in an office. Her Spanish is pretty good, excepting irregular verbs. She will be happy there, planted in the noisy rush of the second-world city—buying dresses, eating sopapillas, sending faxes for her job at the office. In the late afternoons, she'll lie down on the terrace of their hacienda and doze while Max goes to play with his amigos down the street. In the evenings they'll watch television, action shows about banditos with hearts of gold. In one episode the banditos rob an orphanage, but decide, after some deliberation, to stay there and be counselors for a few months. Teresa will turn the television off and several years will pass. The bright, stirring blur of passing years. Max will grow a beard and enormous pectorals. Max will begin to deal narcotics and traffic in child pornography. When Teresa visits him in his filthy Mexican prison cell she'll ask him, "How did this happen?"

"What did you expect?" he'll reply.

The summers will be sticky. Teresa will be transferred to a neighboring firm with a new boss, a beady-eyed man named Jorge who obsessively shines his shoes all day. The smell of black Kiwi polish will pollute the small office. This will go on for months. Finally, Teresa will ask him to open a window. He'll refuse, they'll quarrel violently, and Teresa will accidentally stab him repeatedly with a letter opener. Then she'll look at what she's done in disgust and repent her misliving. She'll flee to New York, her son Max a lost cause now.

In a dismal one-room in Morningside Heights, Teresa will conclude that middle age is unkind. She will notice how her hair sticks up in strange ways, how her skin is pale and blotchy. She'll notice dandruff littering the shoulders of her black jacket: White scattered flake-fall of dandruff on the black jacket. Several desperate years will pass in a parade of odd jobs and long walks. She'll buy a kitten which, in her depression, she'll name Misery.

At the employment agency she will meet a 50-ish man with salt and pepper hair and green eyes. Very striking. She will eye his kind mouth, considering. They'll sit on pillows in an Ethiopian restaurant, scraping up lentils with flat bread. The man will speak in a solid baritone and want to discuss first memories. Teresa will say she doesn't think that's a very good idea. In the restaurant the television plays a made-for-television adaptation of an H.G. Wells story starring actors from a popular action series. Teresa and the man talk about what they would do with a time machine. The man will clamor about going to the future, Teresa will disagree. She thinks, however, she'd like to get to know him, grow old with him, to stay together even when the recession has cost them both their jobs and they are forced to donate limbs to survive and have to prop their amputated torsos up with a complicated system of wires and pulleys and smile at each other across the room.

Wait, Teresa will think to herself, that's horrible.

Teresa will suddenly drop her chapati and rush from the restaurant, hailing a cab in the mean November street. She'll hurry to her room and pack. She'll buy a used car with the returned deposit on her apartment and, with Misery stuffed in a wicker basket, begin to drive west, robbing liquor stores along the way.

Teresa will turn 52 in Kentucky and Kansas, living on Fritos and microwaved chilidogs. She'll speed her red Chevy through cornfields, highways evaporating behind her. She'll sit in a grease-spattered canvas of clothes, a moving utopian chilidog dream. State troopers will screech tires around swamp-logged back roads behind her. Misery will get bigger, sharpen her claws on the dash, shed yellow fur on the vinyl upholstery. In Laramie, Wyoming, Teresa will bury the gun beneath an oleander bush, change the color of her hair, sell the Nova and continue to hitchhike west. Between rides, she'll pore over seminal Buddhist texts, ruminate on the nature of existence, change her cat's name to Bodhisattva.

"That's a weird name for a cat," truckers will say.

She will waitress, she'll swish brushes over dirty dishes; dry hands scrubbing fiercely in several different sinks. At 59, she'll arrive in Oregon and get a job picking lemons. The air will be clean and Teresa will live on seeds and fresh spring water, lunching glorious and carefree in the green Western orchards. Willows will brush her untroubled face. She will close her eyes and dream about the vast, immeasurable universe and all that is about to happen there, of the secret future spread before her that nothing, no matter how true, can undo.

Second Thoughts

I Carry a Hammer in My Pocket for Occasions Such as These

A guy I didn't like approached me on the street. He was wearing a backwards baseball cap and cream-colored jeans. He might have said, "Hey, man, howzitgoing?" He might have said, "Where you headin'" or "You aren't going to believe what happened to me today." I cast him a glance that read rapacious hatred.

He said, "You know why you don't like me, man?"

I said, "Lay it on me."

He said, "The reason you don't like me is because you don't like yourself."

I said, "Is that so?"

He said, "Yeah, perhaps a little sensitivity on your part."

I said, "You think?"

He said, "Yeah, we project onto others our deepest fears and self-loathing."

"You may be right," I said, considering.

We walked awhile together on the street in silence, busses rushing past us. I thought about it. He was right. I knew he was right. After a time the guy asked if he could borrow some money from me. "No problem," I said, and reached in my pocket for the hammer.

Impressions

At a party I met a man made entirely of dots. Tiny dots comprised his face, eyes, and legs. You had to look closely to notice, but they were there. Squinting, you could see his nose didn't quite cohere. We were standing by the snack table holding beer in flimsy paper cups. I chewed a celery stick. We talked, and I studied the logic of his speech. It was possible to sense the space between the things he said. That is, he'd start talking about one thing, then drift to something else. His conversation, like everything, was dots. The dots were different topics, and it was only their proximity to each other that suggested some kind of continuity. I chomped my celery stalk and watched. His cigarette was all in pieces, his hands a speckled mess. Everything about him was loosely related, suggesting a concrete mass. I finished my beer, excused myself, and went looking for the bathroom. The hallway proved difficult to navigate. Perhaps I had misjudged, but it seemed I had just met a man made entirely of dots.

Leaving Places

There was a guy who wanted to leave, always saying so, always telling us, "This is it, I'm really leaving." We said, "Go ahead and do it." "Nothing here is interesting anymore," he told us. We said, "Go."

So he packed his khaki pants, his checkered work shirts, and his *Collected Works of D. H. Lawrence,* and bought a bus ticket to Santa Barbara where his cousin worked in a coffee shop and promised to give him a job: Serving scones, cleaning the coffee grinder.

Two months later, the guy came back. "I never should have left," he said about the place he'd returned to. "Why'd you let me leave?"

The place he'd left where we still were hadn't changed in those two months, or it had changed in such imperceptible ways that you would have needed a magnifying glass to notice.

The more romantically minded among us were curious. "Did you charm the hearts of any young ladies?" we asked. "Oh yeah," the guy said, "I got married." "*Really?*" we said, and made him sit down so he could tell us all about it. "Not much to tell," said the guy. "She was a customer at the coffee shop and when I served her double-latte I said, 'Don't burn your tongue.' After that she kept looking at me over her copy of *Dianetics* and blinking her eyes." "What color eyes?" we asked, and he told us the green of traffic signals.

"Then," he said, "we went on a date to see a Russian play in which the terrible step-father is a drunkard and breaks all the furniture in the house. Then we went to her place and kissed and three days later over a breakfast of omelets I popped the question."

"Any kids?" one of us asked. "I was only there two months, dummy," said the guy who'd left. "Two months is long enough for something to happen," the dummy shot back. "Actually," said the guy, "my wife was pregnant when I left."

One girl, wearing Ben Franklin glasses and a button-up vest—who, incidentally, had also been planning to leave—shouted, "That sounds wonderful, I'm going there." The first guy begged her not to go, but the girl left anyway. She had a cousin who ran a Xerox shop in Santa Monica who promised to give her a job: Changing the toner, collating paper stacks. We got a postcard with a palm tree that read *Having the time of my life.*

Two months later the girl came back. "I never should have left," she said. "Why'd you let me leave?" The first guy who'd left said: "I told you not to go. Are you pregnant?"

To celebrate her return, we took a walk around the town. "Everything looks the same," said the girl. It was true: nothing had changed in her absence, with the exception of a new travel agency and an extravagant rose bush shot with blossoms right outside the firehouse. But you only notice these things if you're paying close attention, the kind of attention you give to a place just before you leave.

And we were all, secretly, planning to leave.

Jane and I at Home One Sunday

For starters, you see, there's Jane and me. It's a fact solid as a parked car, plain as a piece of bread, unshakable as your own skin though some facts are harder to remember than others. We stay home weekends. Every morning I look up to see our cardboard cut-out desk, paper forks and spoons, plastic shirts red, green, gray, and Jane in a dress. Our room is very small, especially when it rains. The clean light on the window is slapped away in gusts. It goes like this:

We wake up in the morning and Jane says hello. I wait for a minute before saying, "Hello."

I try to stand up.

Jane tries to stand up.

Ever seen a room too tiny to stand in, too small even to draw the blinds? The kind of place you spend all day picking lint from the bedspread? We've got it. We look out on the rain and stay mum. It's a divided world where some people have it better, some worse. We leave well enough alone and drink our coffee. Jane's eyes are flat. I don't complain because I'm a waiter. There's a restaurant ten blocks from our house that serves chicken sandwiches, soup, and that's where I work. In the afternoons I walk, put on an apron, pick up a tray, and wait. I bring pastramis and tossed salads while waiting. Thank you, I say, and enjoy yourself.

I get so used to waiting that at home the habit is difficult to break. Sometimes Jane's gone for a few days and I wait fiercely by the phone, expecting rings to fill the room like a flock of injured birds. When Jane is here, I can't even get up for coffee. I hear her in there dropping spoons, breaking cups. Flat Jane is a sharp coffeepot woman in the kitchen.

Jane wears dresses and gestures with her eyes. Green dresses, black eyes. While I wait, I take notes. At the desk in the notebook is me with my pen. I write everything down there. Happy birthday: wrote it down. We're out of butter: wrote it down. Every page in the notebook is scratched out, inked over in X's, cancelled for good. I imagine Jane asking, What are you writing? Scribble, scratch. We're lucky.

Jane was married once to a man named Arnold Metcalf Miller. He was an engineer in some capacity I don't understand. It was recent. Better not to talk about it. Jane says she preferred him to me because he was consistent.

"Don't go back to him!" I beg. "I need you."

She says she doesn't think she will. Besides, he beat her. You think you know trouble?

It's the weekend and it's raining for an ark outside. The roof of the house is getting crushed. Our room grows smaller and twice as humid.

"Go for a walk?" I joke.

"Don't be an ass, my dress will get wet."

I wear a T-shirt. This is Jane and I at home.

At least it's a good building with plumbing, we tell ourselves. Some people have worse. Our room is too small for even bugs to live there. We'd like to look for some, but who has time?

Jane goes in the kitchen with a hairbrush, eyes like raisins. She squishes up her eyes when she looks in the mirror, wrinkles her nose. She's interesting looking for a woman her age. I told her so once. We keep quiet.

No one knocks except the landlord. Name of Fred Dominick with breath like living torture. He told us this was once a good neighborhood, one of the few affordable. We felt lucky. The grocery has pickles, milk, butter. The grocery has sacks of old potatoes. Up five flights we climb with bags. We call our landlord Sewermouth. Rent is $575 with a two-burner hotplate.

"Did you pay Sewermouth this month?" I ask Jane.

"No, I thought you were paying Sewermouth," she says.

Our conversations go on like this. What is there to do? The bugs all left because there was no room to crawl. Our bathroom mirror is in the kitchen.

While Jane makes the coffee, I wear undershirts, waiting. Dressy Jane and T-shirted me. "Don't mention it," she says.

It's Sunday. Some days the quiet is hurricane-like. There's only breathing to be heard and the air gets stiff as cardboard. I know to leave well enough alone.

In the kitchen, Jane drops a spoon.

"For God's sake!" I yell. "I've never heard such a racket!

Jane lets out a strangled laugh like a horse. She drops a drawerful of cutlery on the tile floor; it sounds like an exploding factory. She stands there and laughs, her face gleaming like a tooth.

I run into the kitchen, screaming, "Get out of here with your factory!"

I try to flex my skinny arms over Jane's small horse laughs. Pony laughs. My undershirt is dirty. We look at each other and our eyeballs lock and won't come unstuck. We shiver. As far as I can tell, Jane is upset.

"Why?" she asks aloud.

I wait expectantly. Rain pounds the house.

For a minute Jane says nothing and then says, "Empty, empty."

"Bad as with Arnold Metcalf Miller?" I ask.

She shakes her head.

"Bad as with punches in the gut?"

Jane unbuttons her dress to show off her shiny welts. There are dozens of brownish-blue contusions, puckered as puffed-up mouths. I avert my eyes. The bruises are the color of liver and shine like little signs. All this in the notebook. The letters bleed onto the page, big glaring X's to show where I've been. I want so much to go outside.

"Nothing's perfect," I say.

She knows I'm right and begins to cry.

"I'm no Mister Make Everything A-OK," I admit.

"I know, I know," she sobs. Her raisin eyes squeeze water through thin flesh slits.

I go back to the desk and sit. She knows, and I appreciate that.

"Jane," I say.

She tells me she needs to go to the hospital. I jump up, appreciating the excuse.

"Why?" I ask, "Appendicitis? Tonsillitis? Some-kind-of-itis?"

A scream escapes Jane's teeth.

"Shhhhh," I say, "the neighbors!" She knows as well as me our walls are made of balsa. The neighborhood is old and feeble. Our quiet has kept our contract. Sewermouth thinks we're good, happy kids. It's nothing to mention.

"Jane," I say, "I'm going outside."

Jane screams shrill arrows. I sit fearfully to put on socks. Her dress is still around her waist, mealy chest spilling out all over. Of course, the telephone rings. Jane picks it up, yelling, "Who is it?" In one sock I watch Jane's face go placid as jelly. She holds a hand over the receiver saying, "You know who it is."

"No, I don't," I say, not knowing.

"Yes, yes you do," she says.

I say, "Who?"

"It's Arnold Metcalf Miller."

My stomach rolls like a grind mill. Of course.

"What does he want?" I ask.

"He says he loves me."

Jane's voice is very small. I sit on the bed by the window while rain beats the house like a fist.

"I'm in love with you," I tell her.

"I know you are but what am I?" she says.

"I'm in love with you," I say again.

"I know you are but what am I?"

Jane's voice sounds like it's coming from another century. I look down at my feet. My socks are not clean.

"That's better?" I ask. "You want punches in the gut?"

I make trick fists, holding up two string-limp arms. Jane's face is dead as plaster; her hair hangs over in wiry loops.

"Let me talk," she says.

"You want an engineer in a better neighborhood? If you want we can find a better house, you know."

She says for me to go for a walk, go down six blocks with the apron, tray, and sandwiches, start waiting, and when I come back she'll make toast.

"Just hang up," I say.

"No," she says, "toast."

I put on my shoes and go to the door. She yells at me to go to the store while I'm out. "Pickles and bread," she says. "Take an umbrella." I walk outside and rest my skull on the door. I can hear her talking. Her murmurs sweep after me like the ghost of fingers.

In the street I feel worse. I am shivering T-shirted in the downpour and the streetlamps are snapped in half. Rain and tears get all mixed up. I open the umbrella; its fabric hangs in tatters from a bent metal frame. I'd throw it away, only there are no garbage cans in sight. I imagine myself spending the day curled in a garbage can, tidy cylindrical mausoleum, burning T-shirt and jeans for fuel. Today had started off as Sunday. Who knew?

Get a cab, I tell myself.

I flap my arms and stagger in the rain, singing songs about taxis in a high, whirring voice. One hunches to the curb, its motor turning over. I duck in head-first with my streaming umbrella. The cab driver's face is like a plate of eggs.

"Just drive me around the city," I say to him.

He doesn't respond.

Again, "Just drive me around the city."

Egg-face blinks slowly, his black moustache full as a mop. The inside of the cab is decorated with pinwheels and children's drawings.

I take hold of the driver's head and shout my instructions in his ear. I continue shouting until I realize he is deaf.

I sit back in the seat and say nothing. He accelerates away from the curb and begins driving me around the city.

Three hours pass. I take notes. The pinwheels in the cab turn and I compose writerly lines like, *Whither goes the love-struck fool: a-field, a-far, to mossy, blackened depths,* etc.

"Ugh," I say and scratch them out in my mind. I console myself with the thought of my job waiting, a good building with plumbing, Sewermouth's affordable rent, love's ever-ragged disequilibrium.

"Better off than a lot," I say.

Buildings streak around us in the rain. It's spring, only there are no flowers and the bare branches of trees close in on themselves like fans. You've heard of emptiness? I smile anyway, holding up the corners of my mouth with two fingers.

When we get back to the building, Egg-face tells me the fare is one thousand dollars. I get out my thin, floppy wallet. I remember that I have no money and hold up my hands in good-natured helplessness. I apologize. I dissemble. The driver laughs into his moustache. He smiles, nods and shakes my hand. I embrace him warmly, feeling a surge of immanent brotherhood. He gives me a pinwheel, I give him the warped, useless umbrella. We part the best of friends.

On the curb I see Sewermouth. His plastic slicker is red and blue; the rain makes mist on his thick bifocals.

"Got the rent?" he asks.

I tell him to come and knock tomorrow. I say, "Come and knock," beaming. He thinks we're good, happy kids. Better not to mention.

"How's the Mrs.?" he asks, friendly.

I avert my nose.

"Just fine," I say.

He thinks we're married too. Tomorrow if he comes I'll tell him the wife has the money and isn't in at the moment. Little lies are okay. We'll get it eventually and keep our quiet contract. Worry is my middle name.

"Such good kids," he bubbles, rotten-mouthed.

"Well," I add for good measure, "be seeing you."

"Be seeing you," he says.

I give him the pinwheel. We part the best of friends.

I climb the stairs of my building, searching for my keys. I know I put them in my pocket, only I cannot find my pocket. I am here in the hall imagining bare walls and no one responding to hello, thinking for starters there should be Jane and me. I fall through the door without groceries.

"Hello?" I ask.

In the kitchen I see a note saying I went to the hospital be back soon love jane. You can imagine encouraging? This could mean an end to the overtures of Arnold Metcalf Miller. I am thrilled to the point of confusion. In the bathroom/kitchen mirror there are large, dark circles under my eyes. Black caves, hollow holes. Need to sleep, I tell myself, throwing open cupboards. In the baking dish I put toast. The oven's an inferno. I sling my wet T-shirt on a hook above the stove.

When I go to the bed I try to straighten myself out but keep curling into a spring. I turn there, wiry and wound, trying to relax. The phone rings bloody murder. This is my job, to listen and wait. Have I brought the right thing? In my fingers and toes, anxiety blossoms like tiny flowers. Rain crushes the roof so it comes down around me, cozy as an envelope. My brain is full of bric-a-brac: Hairs in the carpet, moments of impurity, living in a bad neighborhood-- there are worse things. I think: Jane. The darkness has teeth. Shadows smother me to sleep.

Later, I hear her voice, not too distorted by whispers, say she is there. I see her in the room, standing, walls around her like a jacket.

I sit up and say, "Hello."

Her breath cuts warm gullies in the air. I stay very silent. Finally I ask, "What about you know who?"

We don't have to say his name. Do we have to repeat everything?

She says that's nothing.

"You're staying?"

She says, "Shhhhhh, the neighbors."

I say, "Shhhhhh, the neighbors."

We were right with each other.

"What about the phone?" I ask.

"Don't answer."

"The hospital?"

She unlatches her dress and shows me bandages. White gauze held in place by X's of surgical tape. We gape. You think you've understood something after forever of trying to figure it out? We were lucky.

The toast is done and the smell of brown bread paints a spell on the house. She comes to bed in her undone dress and I hold her in my arms like a piece of crumpled paper. We say love. We say need. We say we get the picture.

"Do you promise?" I ask.

"What?"

"What?"

I whisper for her to forget it, crossing out lines in my mind. Some things are better not to mention.

The telephone rings and rings. We ignore it. We tell each other, then, it is safe to cry until we run out of tears, even if we never run out of tears. Our bodies crack like static in the growling dark.

A Telephone Conversation with My Father

When I spoke with my father he said, "How's everything going?" and I said, "Everything's going very well," and he said, "How's the weather?" and I said, "The weather has been fine, Dad, just fine," and he said, "Well, have you been keeping yourself busy?" and I said, "Oh yeah, I've really had a lot of work lately—I've been so, so busy; I've just been doing lots of things, so many things, you know." He said, "Well, I'm glad to hear it." And then I said, "Remember that time after you and Mom were divorced and I hurled a cup of coffee at your head and the cup shattered against the wall permanently staining the white plaster like the blood of a sacrifice?" "Oh yeah," he said, "that was a good one." And then he said, "Remember that time when you were fifteen and you cowered in the corner, then lashed out at me with your fists shrieking that you hated me and you wished you'd never been born?" "I sure do," I assented, "oh, but those were the good ole days." And then I said, casually, "How about all those years you lied to me, Dad," and he yawned and said, "Gosh, it's getting late," and I said, "Yeah I've got to get to bed myself, big day tomorrow, you know," and he said, "Well, I'll let you go then; thanks for calling, son, and I miss you." I said, "You miss me as much as a knife in your side, Dad." "A-ha, that's a good one, son," he chuckled, and hung up.

The Task

I spend a lot of time dreaming about the future, which is one of the reasons I keep forgetting to clean the bathroom. You remind me, sharply, but still I'm here on the couch, pondering options. In the future, I tell myself, I'll get up earlier, pay for everything at the grocery store, and carry all the bags myself. Twice a week I'll bring home surprises: rented movies, stolen rhododendrons, half-price fruit pies. You'll arrive to find the bathtub's been scrubbed with steel wool by me. The whole upstairs will smell of Ajax. Fixtures will glitter like just-thrown confetti, surprising the eye. It's clear I've worked hard:

"Wow," you'll say. "Elbow grease."

Afterwards, it's August, and we'll sit outside in lawn chairs, eating corn on the cob in the sun. Then, in that chair—kernels in my teeth, my heart unknotted at last—I'll look up to see that the past has amended each simple, destructive mistake. And that everything I didn't do I've done.

Invention of the Offenbach

He came out of the barbershop sporting a flat top, pleased that the day was so sunny. "Okay, but why?" His wife crossed paths with a primitive religionist who wielded a snake that sucked copper from her blood. "Okay, but why?" The paramedic ran to a phone booth, fishing around in his jacket for a quarter, which he found, flipped, and dropped in the pocket of his brown, flannel trousers. "Okay, but why?" We'd stumbled from the forest at dawn that day, clothes ragged, hair a rat's nest of burs and twigs, our eyes wild with a wisdom so acute, so richly articulated that we made a beeline for the diner to buy ourselves some cheesesticks. "Okay, but why?" At the house an hour later, the spigots gleamed with a critical malice and someone, a child perhaps, moaned softly in the carport. "Okay, but why?" We remembered our ancestors sold flowers for a printing press, and when their memories were raped by interpretation they remained calm, took baths, and ate toast overlooking the park until the negative element dispersed and the air was alive with ions. "Okay, but why?" Because we answer to whatever name is salvaged coming home from the party: our barrettes left by the empty glass on the nightstand where the light blinks off and hair goes unfastened like money from the bank, a hand to hold. "Okay, but why?" Because this need for connection ties inevitably to absence, and that grass sprouts everywhere, and the clouds are very tall.

Accident by Escalator

I ride the subway every day but I am a distracted man. Carrying my briefcase, watching for my stop, I think about money, the future, primitive religion, and the personal quest. My head is an excited jumble of ideas. Subway lights flash by, stations evaporate. The flux of getting in and out. It is difficult, sometimes, to pay attention to the small things. Escalator stairs move quickly and you have to step off at just the right moment.

I didn't.

The tip of my shoe got caught in the treads and I was slurped down through the grating. My legs went first and then the rest of me, pressed flat into the griddled surface of the metal. Squished in this way, I continued along the dark underside of the escalator.

While I was in there I thought about my life and the nature of fate. I wound around at the bottom and squeezed through the gratings. I peeled myself up. It didn't hurt much. My body, oddly, maintained the shape of spiky corrugation, and was split with four creases where the stairs separate. I was a pancake-flat accordion man.

"I had an accident," I told my girlfriend when I got home. She turned around and looked at me a long minute. My skin was the color of dirty metal.

"What happened?" she said.

When I told her, she asked if I'd been paying attention. I shrugged.

"That's what you get," she said.

I slapped down on the carpet of our apartment. My girlfriend took a rolling pin and tried to smooth me out. It tickled. She put her mouth over my mouth and blew, trying to pop me into three dimensions.

"It's no use," she said eventually.

I thought the change suited me. My torso was a thin, lined slice, my head a pressed plate of ridges. I wove around people, unnoticed, thinking about false fronts, social games, our second selves. Everything seemed easier. In the subway I stood by the wall, near the advertisements. Each day, while exiting, I'd lie down on the escalator and ride it around to maintain my shape. At work they called me Flat Man, Rumpleboy. They barely even noticed I was there. I had my ideas.

Day by day I got used to it, moved with more grace, greater stealth. I wore gray clothes and hunched over at the movies. I ran through the world on thoughts alone: Lao-tzu's butterfly, the adaptability of rock. At night, in bed, I could barely touch my girlfriend. I slept pressed against the wall, curled into my edges. "I can't take this anymore," she said, and moved away.

I was sad. I saw myself getting thinner in the mirror. I shushed and coiled my edges through all parts of the city, thinking about sadness, repetition, and the cyclical nature of things. I looked at myself and said, "Accidents will happen."

Time passed and things got better. I met a doormat named Rebecca. Her jacket was fluffed and matted and there were wet footprints all over her face. We treated each other well, discussing ideas. Happiness became us. We slid very noiselessly beneath each other's feet.

The New Duchamp

The New Duchamp comes over in a jacket made of curds, flecked with dark, running smears, and smelling like an athlete's unwashed crotch. He calls it his "blue cheese look."

When I say hello he slaps me in the face. When I say, "Try to be reasonable," he whips out a bassoon and commences "We are the Champions." He takes from my cabinets aspirin, socks, handkerchiefs, and fifty dollar bills. The New Duchamp pontificates on the irrefutable value of stealing for artistic reasons.

"Come in and make yourself at home," I say. He leaves. Immediately, he knocks again. I open the door. "What do *you* want?" he asks me. When I stare at his face, he looks at the ceiling. When I look at the ceiling, he leans forward and kisses me. "Are you coming in or aren't you?" I ask. He runs around to the side of the building and jumps in through the window carrying a cellophane bag full of gerbils. "What are you doing here?" he demands. When I tell him there's German food for dinner, he puts his foot through the television. The New Duchamp pontificates on the irrefutable value of gerbils.

Using my pots, my stove, my noodles, my strainer—the New Duchamp cooks a monstrous plate of spaghetti. As soon as it's finished he rushes to the stairwell and throws it over the banister. He calls this piece: Food Descending A Staircase.

The New Duchamp's goal is to out-Duchamp the original. "I am more Duchamp than Duchamp," he claims. In a fit of zeal he makes a free-standing sculpture out of clothespins, a potato, and a piece of lint. He dances Swan Lake on his hands. The New Duchamp says his favorite organ is the pancreas and shows me the one he keeps in his pocket for fondling. "The pancreas!" he cries, "Irrefutably valuable!"

The New Duchamp rolls to the store and buys fifty rivets. He lies in my bathtub and cries, "We're here! We're here!"

At dinner, the New Duchamp is not decorous. He pretends to snore loudly whenever I speak. He puts strudel down his pants, then blinds himself biting into a bratwurst. I understand he's nervous because tonight is the big exhibition. He explains to me how he'll burst onto the scene. In his new piece, he says, he'll outdo Duchamp's famous urinal installation by appearing at the exhibition as a total unknown and urinating on the exhibition's visitors.

At the event, I am dressed in a jacket and tie and the New Duchamp is wearing his cheesecoat. As the New Duchamp prepares his exhibition, security guards rush in and begin to pummel him with nightsticks.

"Perfect! Perfect!" he shouts between laughs.

"New Duchamp," I ask timidly, "why are you laughing?"

"Even as dark is our bridesmaid," he replies, as the guards go on beating him and he goes on laughing.

Goodbye Now

My heart is set to detonate into a thousand pieces. I am on the train, in my uniform, leaving my future wife to go to war. Her name is Rebecca, and she is across from me in the train compartment, which is no bigger than a telephone booth. The tiny space of the car makes saying goodbye impossible. My dog Pernicious is crammed in with us. "He's more like a goat, really," says Rebecca, and she's right.

Rebecca has on silver earrings and a green dress. Her black eyes shine like a sad breeze through olive trees. "You look so beautiful," I keep telling her, my own eyes wet and burning. Distraught, I fiddle with the buttons of my soldier's coat. I balance my hat on my knee and look at a spit-shined shoe. At war, my chest will glitter with medals and I'll be made an officer before coming back to live out my life in a wooden house with Rebecca, raising a family, growing old.

But that is a thousand years away. This moment is goodbye now. The dog's long, Angora-like coat keeps getting in Rebecca's mouth because the train compartment is so small, and Rebecca is saying "Pernicious is a problem," while the dog keeps standing up, lying down, licking our faces, and whimpering pathetically. He knows one of us is leaving, and the melancholy is driving him insane.

The Vow of I Never
Want to Open My Eyes

Getting Older

I fell asleep and dreamt for a very long time. Meanwhile, movers came into my house and picked up the easy chair and the stereo, and all of my kitchenware including the spatula, can opener, carrot peeler, corkscrew; also the Formica table, and many books which they might have put in plastic bags and carried out by hand.

I woke up and said: "What happened?" I usually say this on waking, but this morning it was different. Immediately I called my friend Joshua.

"Joshua," I said, "who's responsible?"

"Ha," Josh said. "You've been asleep forever!"

"Why?" said I, "what'd I miss?"

"You're not even asking the right questions," Josh laughed, and hung up.

Befuddled, I rubbed my eyes. I went into the bathroom to splash water on my face, but the movers had taken the water. I combed my hair with my thumbnail, then drifted to the kitchen to make myself some toast. I found bread, but the movers had taken the toaster.

"No toaster!" I yelled.

Then—in my sleepy-headed, not-too-quick way—I began to understand. The rooms were filled with wind. It was going to be a day without toast. Before me was no breakfast, no chairs to sit on; that sweet, stolen music would never start my mornings. I knew I was getting older, but I never imagined it would be this *difficult*.

The Enigma of Possibility

Derek had lost his job and was wondering where the rent would come from. Then he sat on the bed and ate a tangerine. His tongue worked round and round in a frenzy of tasting. His tongue was the longest tongue in the world. It was an extraordinary tongue. In his pocket there was a special tongue brush and a pair of tongue tweezers and his little blue tube of special chalky cleanser. He tried seeing if he could touch the wall with his tongue from the bed. He tossed the tangerine up in the air and, using only his tongue, caught it with a flourish. *There must be some way I can get money for the rent,* Derek thought, *but how?*

Allegorical Story with Literal Window

First they were giants inside a tiny room. All around them were miniature newspapers, miniature teacups, miniature picture frames and dictionaries. When she shifted position, her knuckles struck the table. He came to her, putting foreshortened flowers in a miniature vase, then nodded, eating miniature food.

"Maybe we should move," he said, but they never did.

Years passed. They paced the floor with hunched shoulders, and bent double to escape the ceiling, which pressed down on them like a giant white hand. She slouched on the miniature sofa and tried to relax. He listened to small music on a miniature cassette.

"Let me tell you about my day," she said, but it was no use acting normal. He said, "Let's just keep quiet until lunch time," but lunch, according to the miniature clock on the wall, was hours away.

By then their hunger was so fierce that they were getting smaller too: legs, hands, and hearts bit by bit diminished, the air leaking out—a balloon going dead. That's what it was like: a bird in a box, still breathing.

Soon, so softly it was impossible not to listen, she said, "We've lived here too long." In recognition their eyes searched nervously at the walls. Their one-inch arms waved out, cracking corners. They conferred: by then they'd grown so small it seemed they might slip out the miniature window. Her fingers fumbled at the latch, and the latch dissolved, like gasoline. With what strength their baby legs could offer they hoisted themselves to the sill and cast one more look behind. Then at last, with mouths nearly vanished in a tiny patch of face, they said their goodbyes and escaped.

Nothing Bad Happens Here

It's Sunday. I'm happy. My back is to the library and I'm facing the square of the little town I live in. Paid assistants wheel invalids in wheelchairs. Teenaged girls hold hands and laugh. Me? I gasp. There's something in my throat. I cough to dislodge it, but nothing. I hack. An old lady with a hunched back smiles. The sun paints the Town Hall a buttery gold. I hold my neck. The thing in my throat is a pen cap, maybe, or the end of a very old breadstick. Worse things have happened. A string-thin air stream whistles through the object. I take two unsteady steps and double over. Do I worry? The pavement's sort of filthy. Some gum is stuck in a spit-mottled glob over there. Ice cream trucks round the corner, tinkling music. A couple comes out of a clothing store. I hail the police, but there are no police—There's nothing to fix here: every crisis passes. I observe the ass of a horse crossing the street in a processional. There's a parade today! Flamenco dancers on a hay-covered cart. It's a lovely little town. I go down on one knee. An involuntary wheeze strains my faceplate. A dog I don't recognize nuzzles my hairline and the world curls and crackles at the edge. Red dots erase the marching band. I opt for a nap on the concrete by the newsstand while this afternoon repeats itself, endlessly assuring. Where we live there is no mercy. A bright, yellow zeppelin hangs high on the skyline. Blackbirds are perched on the church.

I Bring the Lip Balm

Ever since he scaled the heights of Machu Picchu, my shadow has had a cocky way about him. From my room I see him strutting around in a pair of fancy pants. On the opposite wall his shape looms large, then surges, shrinks to a dot along the corridor tile, and ends at the mirror where he clips his chest hair with a pair of little scissors. I know everything about him. My shadow's favorite food is baked beans, and on the day of my barbecue he eats three cans worth as he cruises the lawn, talking to the ladies. My shadow spends all day at the barbecue, never once crushed by the Hibatchi. I try coaxing him to go, but he just leans back in a lawn chair, playing the harmonica. Finally I have to escort him off the premises—dragging him, literally, by his flickering hair. Playing dead is another attribute my shadow has. His sleepy voice sounds like he's gargling with gravel. "Am I in bed yet?" he asks. "Asleep?" Back in his room, my shadow frightens me by taking out a porcupine quill he claims to have inherited from his father and sliding it, very carefully, into his chest. Says this cleans the sludge from his heart. My shadow is forever tapping against the quasi-permeable membrane of the self. "Who are you *really*?" I ask, looking straight into his face. He says, "If you want to know who, you are doomed," then goes on to complain that his lips are real chapped.

Second Nature

I spent most of Monday morning vacuuming the house in my pajamas, thinking about how ritual becomes second nature. How we floss each tooth without concentrating, for instance; how karate students bow to the master when they're worried about the math test. How flatly I said I loved you, mornings wrapped together in the sky-colored quilt whenever our room was cold. Midwestern winters made it so cold you could sometimes see your breath. My chin fit your shoulder like a seesaw, and I'd watch the breath slipping into your ear, then say it, casually as asking you to pass the pepper.

At that time we lived in a two-story house, and vacuuming the stairs was difficult. You had to yank the cord, and lug the whole thing on the landing where cobwebs clogged up the fuzzy black nozzle. Cleaning is a ritual. We'd always be down on our knees with the Dust Buster, or upstairs scrubbing the sink. It's essential to scrub all the old dirt away, so you can make plenty of room for the new dirt. These activities: scouring rust spots, upending dresser drawers. Then to put everything in order, which took all day, upstairs and down.

My house now is much smaller. I can vacuum it in the time it takes for my ripped stereo speakers to start getting on my nerves. The showery hiss of static like snow. The room is sliced right to the core. I shiver, even in pajamas, even deep down in my sheepskin slippers. Every time I said those things, I swear to you, I meant it. I mean I did not miss a breath.

Gainesville, Oregon — 1962

Afternoon at the Gilberts. 3:00 P.M. September light slants through the dappled leaves of the apple bough. Stephen is fourteen, a freshman in high school. He sits by the window puzzling over math equations, a pencil gripped in his sweaty fist. One of these variables is divisible by three. Though Stephen's grooming habits are generally excellent, his fingernails are raw, spiky, chewed to a frazzle. He is nervous because his future, which seems to him imminent, is an irreducible unknown. The math test is tomorrow.

To Stephen's sister Janice, recently sixteen and satisfied with her C in Geometry, the math test is of no concern. Janice is on the sun deck, combing her hair in the manner of supremely confident teenaged girls. She is listening to the radio and chewing gum. The black comb moves through her hair with a crackle of electricity. The trick to popularity, Janice believes, is to have the right attitude. Be assertive, and try not to dwell on your own imperfections. Janice's teeth are a bit bucked, but not much.

The song on the radio is "Don't Fall In Love With A Stranger" by Ricky Nelson. Over the gnarled, leafy branches of the apple bough, across the street from the Gilberts', a neighbor, Mr. Flanigan, is making a racket mowing his lawn with a motorized mower. Janice has to turn up the volume on the radio to hear Ricky Nelson at all.

Outside, across the four-way-stops of Gainesville, not far from the Gilberts' house, Kevin Dougherty is approaching in a silver Impala. Kevin is seventeen and a tenor in the school's barbershop quartet. The pockets of his letterman's jacket are filled with crushed packs of gum. On Gainesville's residential streets, Kevin does not obey the speed limit. He winds the silver Impala past lawns clipped closely as poodles, speeds to the Texaco for gas, stops at the flower shop to buy Janice a red rose wrapped in white tissue. A witty remark passes between Kevin and the flower shop cashier. She smiles politely. The trick to being well liked is to ingratiate yourself socially. Kevin snaps along in a crisp shirt, laced tennies, hair shorn to a smart flattop. Kevin and Janice have a date to go to the bowling alley. Kevin is Janice's boyfriend and the math teacher's son.

At the high school Kevin's father, Mr. Dougherty, the math teacher, is still meeting students after class, explaining equations, searching blank student faces for a flicker of comprehension. Mr. Dougherty's forehead shines under fluorescent lights. His students duck their heads to avoid blasts of hour-old pastrami sandwich breath. The students try not to snicker at the chalk prints on his khakis. Mr. Dougherty wonders if this is the meaning of being an adult. Mr. Dougherty likes his job, except when he thinks about it—which he does, from a sense of self-preservation, not often.

The front door to the Gilberts' house is open and Mrs. Gilbert, Stephen and Janice's mother, is making meatloaf sandwiches in the kitchen. All around, the gleam of the Gilberts' kitchen tiles reflects well-washed pots and the spice rack gives the impression of a grand, enviable orderliness. The vinyl chairs have been wiped since breakfast. Mrs. Gilbert believes that the trick to a good meatloaf sandwich is to use plenty of ketchup. You pound the bottom of the bottle until the bread is wet and ruddy. Everyone loves it.

In the room next to the kitchen, at the table by the window, Stephen is still sitting with his head buried in the math book. The math book, titled *Solutions for a Better Future*, has a picture of a rocket on the cover. Stephen's teeth worry his frazzled fingernails. If only he understood polynomials! He'll never get into Northwestern at this rate. The math test is tomorrow.

Stephen's cat, Esmeralda, a calico with one working eye, slinks to a dish by the door and gnaws a row of bones there. Like Stephen, Esmeralda has a nervous disposition. Her condition is quite advanced, even for a cat.

Just now there is a knock at the Gilberts' door. It is Traci,

65

Janice's best friend. Mrs. Gilbert comes to the door wiping her hands on her apron, wondering if her bones can take much more of this standing, this walking and opening of doors. Mrs. Gilbert pushes the screen. She is pleased but not surprised to see Traci because Traci comes over quite often.

"Hi, Mrs. Gilbert!"

"Hi, Traci! I just finished making some meatloaf sandwiches. They're in the fridge if you want one."

"Oh, thanks, Mrs. Gilbert, but I'm just here to see Janice."

"Well, she's out on the sundeck."

Traci's red sweater is made of expensive cashmere. Her heeled shoes give her steps an insistent click.

On the sundeck, Janice is still pulling the black comb through her blonde, often-washed hair. Traci runs her fingers through her own hair, which is wavy and black. Traci thinks she is prettier than Janice because her freckles, she believes, give her face a funny, distinctive charm. Traci wishes *she* were Kevin Dougherty's girlfriend instead of Janice. Traci thinks Kevin Dougherty is a total dreamboat. She'd like to ride beside him in the silver Impala, laugh at his jokes, muss his flattop.

"Hi, Janice!"

"Hi, Traci!"

Over the apple tree's branches, from across the street, the buzz of Mr. Flanigan's mower cuts the air. This is Gainesville, Oregon, 1962. These are lives laid out, like lawns, with geometrical precision and kept with great care. Of course, Janice knows that Traci likes Kevin, and Traci knows that Janice knows. Best friends are like that.

"Kevin and I have a date to go to the bowling alley," says Janice, smacking gum.

"Oh," Traci says, "can I come too?"

"I guess so," says Janice, with a giggle.

At school, in the math classroom, the light off Mr. Dougherty's forehead hurts the eyes of Stephen's friend Louis. Louis furrows his brow, feigning concentration. Mr. Dougherty is giving Louis an after-school tutorial on polynomials.

"Pay attention," Mr. Dougherty instructs. The math book, *Solutions for a Better Future*, is open on the desk between them. Louis is wearing an orange windbreaker. Eruptions of acne cover his face. His parents think he is Ivy League material but Louis, like Stephen, is only fourteen and feels he is too young to know yet. Louis has an extremely low sense of self-esteem.

Kevin Dougherty screeches his Impala to a halt in the Gilberts' driveway. He gets out in his crisp shirt, holding the red rose. Mrs. Gilbert hears the knock on the door, but refuses to acknowledge it. Not one more, she tells herself. She goes into the living room where Stephen is bent over the math book in frustration, hands gathering fists of hair.

"I'm going up to my room for awhile, Stephen," she says. "If you get hungry, there are some meatloaf sandwiches in the fridge." She winks. "With ketchup." Mrs. Gilbert makes herself a drink, climbs the stairs, and closes the door to her bedroom.

Kevin Dougherty knocks again, then opens the screen, calling: "Hello?" Esmeralda the cat darts from her food dish and runs out the opened door. Kevin comes in, calling Janice's name. Stephen looks up from the math book and tells Kevin that Janice is out back. Since Kevin is Janice's boyfriend, he comes over quite often. Kevin goes out to the sun deck.

"Hi, Traci," he says, surprised.

Ricky Nelson is playing on the radio. Kevin thinks Traci's freckles are cute, but he is so in love with Janice's somewhat bucked teeth. He gives Janice the red rose wrapped in white tissue paper.

"You're so sweet!" Janice says, and kisses him on the lips. Traci is jealous. Kevin blushes, pleased with himself. "Ready for the bowling alley?" he asks.

Frustrated by the pointless tutorial with Mr. Dougherty, Louis climbs on his bike and pedals out of the high school parking lot in the direction of Stephen's house. Louis's head is crammed with meaningless equations. His orange windbreaker billows in the breeze. He feels certain that he will fail the math test, certain that he will never amount to anything. Likewise, at his house, Stephen gets up from the dining room table with a sigh of abject resignation. It is possible that polynomials will ruin his future. He sits down on the couch and tunes into *This Is Your Life* on T.V.

"I think Traci wants a kiss, too," Janice says, coyly. Kevin blushes, then leans over and kisses Traci lightly on the lips. Traci's heart beats heavily against her red cashmere sweater. Her mouth catches Kevin's as he starts to pull away. She holds him there. The sundeck is protected by high wooden walls, and no one can see in.

Louis thunks down his bike's kickstand and knocks at the Gilberts' door. No one answers, so he lets himself into the living room and slumps on the couch next to Stephen. Louis is depressed. He scratches at his acne.

"I don't know if I can take it anymore," he says.

Stephen says he knows what he means.

"No, really," Louis says, "I just don't think I can stand it."

"Alright already," says Stephen.

In her room, Mrs. Gilbert drinks her drink and thumbs through the New Testament.

"For everyone who asks, receives; and he who seeks, finds; and to him who knocks, it shall be opened," she reads aloud, to no one.

Mr. Dougherty locks his classroom. His mind is filled with images of slack, expressionless student faces. The secret to a sense of well-being, he believes, is not to think too much about things. He walks to the parking lot, gets into his Bonneville, and heads home.

On *This Is Your Life*, a man is reunited with his long lost half-brother.

"But that kind of thing could never happen in real life," Stephen tells Louis.

Stephen and Louis get up from the couch and sneak to the hall to steal some quick sips from the Gilberts' liquor cabinet. A quick sip of brown stuff. A quick sip of clear stuff. Across the street, Mr. Flanigan's mower whirs like a furious insect.

Kevin is still kissing Traci, both of them caught in the sudden, surprised thrill of it. Janice giggles, smacking her gum. She eases Kevin's letterman's jacket from his shoulders. The pockets of the jacket hold gum and a pitch pipe. Kevin knows all the starting pitches to "Coney Island Baby." Janice slips her hands around his waist.

Esmeralda the cat is chased from an opened garbage can by a pack of dogs. She screeches. She is such a nervous cat.

Mrs. Gilbert takes several tranquilizers and lies down on the bed to rest. A doctor prescribed the tranquilizers, so it's nothing to worry about. "Something to relax you," the doctor had said. Mrs.

Gilbert takes several more for maximum relaxation. She finishes her drink. As she tunnels into sweet and gauzy sleep, Mrs. Gilbert hears music through the open window. Is that an angel singing? No, it's Ricky Nelson.

Mr. Dougherty loves his Bonneville. He rolls past lampposts, lawn furniture, clusters of wooden mailboxes. He remembers buying the Bonneville some six years before: how the interior had gleamed, how its first tank of gas cost twenty cents a gallon. Kevin was only a boy then. Youth bloomed in everyone's body. It's better not to dwell in the past. But if we could only turn back the clock, Mr. Dougherty thinks, turning the Bonneville's steering wheel.

Stephen and Louis slump against the liquor cabinet, laughing, a bottle of Mrs. Gilbert's bourbon between them. They feel light and slightly dizzy. When Louis laughs, his teeth grind together. The tension is tight as a tourniquet.

On the sundeck, no one speaks, but breathing is punctuated by sounds of surprise. Janice massages the lump in Kevin's jeans. Traci's breasts fall free as she unclasps her bra. She lifts her red cashmere sweater off with a scissoring of arms. Canned applause from *This Is Your Life* erupts from the television in the living room.

Stephen and Louis decide to climb onto the roof with the bottle of bourbon. They shimmy from Stephen's bedroom window, easing out over the layered shingles, navigating hot tar with hands and feet. Louis is laughing a little, crying a little.

"What do you think would happen if we jumped from here?" Louis asks, brow furrowed in concentration.

In the bedroom, Mrs. Gilbert's heart slows to a thick, ethereal thudding. To her own distant ears, it sounds like the music of an immanent arrival, the coming of something too-long neglected and shot through with light. Maybe I won't cook dinner tonight, she thinks. Let them, this once, fend for themselves.

Three intersections away, Mr. Dougherty pulls the Bonneville through a stop sign, equidistant from the school to his house. Remembering Louis's pimpled face, Mr. Dougherty considers quitting his job.

The sundeck is a frantic tangle of straps and fabrics. Janice is bent over a lawn chair, underwear around her ankles. Kevin's fingers work up inside her. His Levis are unsnapped, unzipped.

Over the roof of the house, the math test looms before the two boys bigger than their future, it laughs like an end to their lives. A polynomial is a function of two or more summed terms, each term consisting of a constant multiplier and one or more variables raised, in general, to integral powers. That should be easy to understand. Traci puts her mouth around Kevin's stiff cock. He holds her head, watches her freckles bob, twists a hand in her dark, wavy curls.

Esmeralda, still chased by the dogs, darts from the curb into the street. The dogs have terrible teeth. They bark. Across the street, on the other side of the apple tree, Mr. Flanigan turns off the motorized mower and the machine shudders to a hush.

Mr. Dougherty rounds a corner perpendicular to the Gilberts' house. He sees a flash in the road, a bright blur of calico, and screeches the Bonneville's brakes.

Shaky-limbed, Louis edges toward the roof's ledge.

"Probably just break a leg," Stephen tells him. Louis asks Stephen to pass him the bottle. Stephen does. It is important to help your friends.

Kevin pulls away and lies flat on the hot surface of the sundeck. Traci, sprattle-legged, lowers herself onto his face while Janice, knees locked around his hips, begin to pump up and down. Slowly at first, then faster.

Mr. Dougherty swerves the wheel but not soon enough to miss Esmeralda, who rolls beneath the tires with a sickening crunch. The dogs whimper from the curb. Mrs. Gilbert's breath is coming full and slow, slow and full enough to fill the sails of a boat.

Louis turns to reach for the bottle and one of his sneakers slips from the roof into the rain gutter, which gives immediately with a rusty crack, releasing a violent confetti of early autumn leaves. Louis pitches out, away from the house.

Kevin, Traci and Janice come suddenly, in succession, with barely audible whimpers: Traci bumping against a moving tongue and mouth, Kevin and Janice milking a tight, grinding channel. Louis tumbles head over feet, past the sundeck, and lands in the hedges bordering the back of the house. The television blares.

Mr. Dougherty gets out of his Bonneville and takes a quick, horrified look beneath his wheels. He knows Esmeralda is the Gilberts' cat. What will little Stephen say? He'll be crushed! Mr.

70

Dougherty feels terrible. He walks toward the Gilbert's porch to tell the family what happened. He rings the doorbell.

Hearing the doorbell, Kevin, Traci and Janice disentangle themselves, scrambling for their clothes. Behind the closed door of her bedroom, Mrs. Gilbert is slipping to the lip of a coma. In her wavering sphere of light, she cannot hear the doorbell. On the roof, Stephen is staring down at his friend's motionless body sprawled in the hedges. He cannot hear the doorbell. Mr. Flanigan, raking leaves in the yard across the street, cannot hear it either.

Kevin, Traci and Janice run clickity-clack in heels and unlaced tennies around the side of the house, hop in the Impala and peel out, leaving skid marks across the Gilbert's blacktop driveway. They tear toward the bowling alley, ignoring the speed limit. Kevin is an excellent bowler. Rows of white pins will shortly be obliterated. Janice brushes her hair and Traci sings along with the radio. It's Ricky Nelson.

Even through the cheap Impala speakers, Ricky Nelson's voice is sensual and soft as butter. An electric guitar, as if from another planet, sends messages, and Ricky Nelson's voice swirls up through the branches of Gainesville's giant apples and oaks, his tone a wisp of smoke warning you, baby, to not fall in love with a stranger, because that could be dangerous. You're so sweet and innocent, what would happen to you then? Please, please, he whispers, come back home.

Dan Meets Dave

Dan, have you met Dave? Dave, this is Dan. Dan, Dave.

Dave said he thought he might have met you before, but Dan you've never seen Dave before in your life, have you? I didn't think so. Must have been some other Dan who looked like you. Anyway— Dave, Dan—I'm sure you'll have plenty to talk about. Dave's been thinking about restoring his antique tractor and entering it in the Lualiafield tractor contest, Dan, and since your antique tractor is a shining example of restoration, and seeing as how you won the Lualia last year, I thought you might could give Dave some pointers. That's a convo sparker right there.

And Dave, Dan's got a baseball card collection that is not to be believed. Dan's got doubles of Carl Yastremski and Dave I know you need a Carl Yastremski, and Dave I know you've got doubles of Joe Rudi from the Oakland A's and Dan I know you've been searching high and low for a vintage Joe Rudi. I've got a feeling you two are gonna hit it off big.

Dave, did you know that Dan's favorite band is the Flying Burrito Brothers? And Dan—guess what?—Dave lives for those little pimento sandwiches. It's kinda uncanny, really. Like predestination.

Dan, maybe Dave can help you reinforce the steel and concrete infrastructure for the underground fitness facility you're building beneath your summerhouse? Dave's great at handiwork, and he's got his own cement mixer 'cause he put up a personal squash court at Springvale last year. An epic meeting: Dan and Dave.

Hey, Dan once broke three vertebrae trying to do a standing flip, Dave, same as you. I'm getting chills from the connective energies at large here. Speaking of chills: Dan? If your wife's still looking for a little extra something on the side, the proportions of Dave's pulsating column of manhood are legendary. Although maybe I could help out a little in that department too. Heh-heh. Heh. Eh-heh-heh-heh. Eh-heh-heh.

Hoo.

Either of you got a buck for the jukebox?

The Weather Retires

It happened quickly, when no one was expecting it. The weather sat down in an easy chair to rest. Soon there was no sun. Not much later, rain disappeared. The sky put up chrome-colored shutters for silence; so silence, except a few clouds that groaned like old plumbing.

I'd just hung up the phone with you and was waiting, drinking water. When I listened out the window a passing blizzard hiccupped.

On my porch a dog scratched fiercely at the screen—maybe he craved water, or lacked the touch of love. I liked his shrouded, off-brown eyes, but my arm couldn't reach. In the post-weather world, would petting be permitted? I rubbed a cloth across my face, but was not comforted.

Skeletal trees shook twigs at me. Darkness surged and slept. Even the glass in my hand was gradually emptied as the air got drier and drier until there was nothing left to eat but my own brain. One white-gray life away, I still can taste the image of you in your house, me in mine—completely ash-covered by the afternoon's end.

That Which I Should Have Done, I Did Not Do

Because it was a party at my house, there was much to be done. Candles were lit, music played. My friend introduced me to his friend, Henry. Henry, this is Anthony, Anthony, Henry. I reached up, shook Henry's hand. I looked him straight in the bespectacled face and nodded. I gave his arm a vigorous, rubbery tug. I smiled. Henry smiled. My friend's eyes flooded over with gratitude and appreciation. Henry and I stood by the doorway and had conversation.

"How's it going?" he said.

"Glad to hear it," he said.

"Really?" he said.

"I totally, totally agree," he said.

I told him to take off his coat and stay awhile.

"Aren't you the perfect host," he quipped. We looked around the room, pretending to admire it.

While Henry and I were getting to know each other, more people arrived. They made the doorbell play its little song. When the door swung open I saw Peggy, Doug, and two girls I didn't know. The girls were wearing T-shirts. I said hello in a voice of pure melting butter. Peggy, high on social graces, immediately offered introductions.

"Anthony, I'd like you to meet Sarah, Sarah this is Anthony, Lynn this is the host, Anthony, Anthony, Lynn."

The space between us was bridged by clasped hands. Sarah and Lynn had nails burnished to a rosy shine. We shook. Their slim fingers crackled beneath mine. Doug made a comment saying: We sure had trouble finding a place to park. Henry was still standing there so I felt obliged.

"Lynn, Sarah, this is Henry."

They asked each other how did they do?

"Peggy," I said, "do you know Henry?" Peggy said she didn't think so.

I said, "Well then, Henry, this is Peggy." They called out Hello! Doug reached over and shook Henry's hand introducing himself. They were both saying nice to meet you when I asked would anyone like anything to drink? Lynn looked around the room, pretending to admire it.

"Where should we put our coats?" Peggy asked.

In the kitchen I whipped up snacks: crackers and cheese-bits, fruit halves, pretzels, carrot strips, celery stalks. Each pierced artfully with a ribbon-topped toothpick. In the living room I could hear laughter. A tall guy with a trimmed beard sidled up by the sink.

"Have we met?" he asked.

My honest answer was I didn't think so and he said I'm Lawrence. His breath was bad.

"Wonderful to meet you!" I said, and offered him a Triscuit. My hand clasped his. He told me he was a friend of Trish's.

"I don't think I've met Trish," I said.

Trish was in the living room. Lawrence introduced us. Arms leapt up like automatons. We laughed the laughs of trivialities acknowledged. It was, after all, my party. We got better acquainted.

"What do you do?" she asked.

"That must be interesting," she said.

I bit into a celery stalk and chewed. She asked if I had met her husband. My fingers jerked, jangling like chandeliers. My hands stayed busy with napkins, the brushing of cuffs. A short, stocky man walked over when Trish gestured.

"Anthony, this is my husband, Wayne. Wayne, this is the host! It's his apartment!"

"Well, I'll be," Wayne said, "I was just admiring it. Do you mind if I ask how much you pay?"

As I was swallowing celery, a hand landed on my back.

"This your apartment?" a guy asked.

"Yes, I'm Anthony," I said. I shook his right hand, his left.

"Well," the guy said, "there's a phone call for you."

Because my hands were full of chilled glass platters bearing vegetables, I asked a long-haired adolescent kid to wedge the phone between my ear and cocked shoulder. I said, "Hello?"

"What's happening over there?" Jane asked.

When I told her I was having a little party, she wanted to know why I hadn't called her. I tried to think of a reason. I tried to think why I hadn't simply picked up the phone and called her. Finally I remembered:

"Oh," I said, "my hands were full."

"What?"

"Oh no!" I said. The receiver slipped from my shoulder and thudded on the carpet. I stood staring, blank as a screen. I couldn't pick it up. The long-haired adolescent kid, sitting nearby, picked up the phone and placed it in the cradle.

"Thanks for helping me out there," I said. "Did we meet?"

Well, the party was splendid and everyone had a pleasant time. Hands were shaken, conversations occurred. "Having a nice time? So many people to meet! We really should be going soon." I whisked about the rooms, busy as a chipmunk, nodding, smiling, leaping to agree. There's always so much to do. At the evening's end I stood at the door and shook hands; I said, "It was nice to meet you" thirty-seven times. The guests got in their cars and drove away. I stood on the porch and waved. I stayed there, even after they'd left, waving like crazy.

That night I had a dream I attended a banquet thrown by a band of rats. The wide room was as blue as a night sky, shot with spectacular waves of gold lightning. The rats brought out the best china; they polished silver and laid a little table with a delicate lace cloth. They set themselves on high stools, whiskers twitching, gnawing their own paws. They sipped lemonade from thimbles. They were dainty rats, they had such manners. In the dream I decided to ask them to stay with me at all times. They accepted just then and climbed in my bed. Their fur was damp and their whiskers tickled. They began to gnaw off my hands. Soon my arms were nothing but two padded lumps, two clapping slabs. In the dream, I knew the rats were right. I stood up in bed and shouted: "Hooray rats, and thank you."

What I'm Doing After This

Mark, my landlord, brought by a bag of green beans. He stood on my front step: glasses, hat. Maybe it was his way of saying, "Glad you paid the rent on time." I snatched the bag and thanked him. Down in the cellar I went with the beans and began to build a time machine. As soon as it's finished I want to blast out of here, because Mark and his wife have problems. They argue all the time. Their house is too close to mine. Sometimes they torture the shih tzu with the garden hose. Coming back from dance class their eyes gleam pure murder, then Susan complains about her ill-proportioned arm, and makes Mark massage her elbow to wrist with 100% olive oil. In the back yard I can see them grappling. "That tickles," she says, as Mark twists her hand behind.

Once they invited me for dinner. Mark didn't know a mango was something you were supposed to eat, and several appliances were smashed. Shortly after, Susan had a hysterical pregnancy. "Causality cannot be held responsible for one thing following another," Mark said. I felt very afraid and excused myself to go home.

In the basement, I went to work on my time machine, and here I am still with my hammer and green beans. It's mysterious: the habits of these people, the terrible sense of sequence. Soon I'll blast off with a speed that will freeze the stars purple. I want to go back to the land of beginnings. I long to break this waking chain.

The Unfortunate Poker Game

The Story of Our Lives

It's like this: What we really want is to drift off in dreams, but life keeps shaking us awake, kicking us out of bed and into the ice cold workplace.

I, for one, decided against it. I put on my best silk shirt and collected every coin in the house. Out on the freeway my Camaro topped 110, slicing through the cornfields of the Midwest at night. Soon state troopers followed, and there was a convoy of lights heading west, the whirl of high sirens. I sped through the canyons and into California, smashing an endless succession of roadblocks.

I knew that if caught, I'd be put behind bars, but I also knew I couldn't keep the chase on forever. Finally, exhaustion got the better of me, and after thirty-five years of high-speed pursuit, I decided to give it a rest.

I pulled the Camaro off the interstate and into the parking lot of a place called The Meek and Sleepy Diner. There were only a few cars there, and not much movement through its misted, silver windows. The Meek and Sleepy Diner sign was not lit up and did not spin.

Save the glow of some candles on the counter, it was dark inside. The air was thick with the smell of people who are close to giving up, but haven't. The cashier, for example, looked on the verge of collapse. A dejected truck driver slurped coffee through a straw. In a booth nearby, two senior citizens leaned their large heads together, drowsing over eggs. I knew I'd come to the right place, and took the booth behind them.

My waitress walked over like her dress was made of lead.

She was an older woman, tall and slouched over. Her half-lidded eyes moved slow over forks and saucers and her left hand, badly mutilated, clutched an order pad and pencil. Her name tag read Rachelle.

"I lost three fingers in a kitchen accident," she said, sliding into my booth.

I nodded.

Rachelle lay her head next to the salt and pepper shakers and shut her eyes. Her freckles looked like someone had scattered a fistful of sand there. The lines by her eyes made tiny constellations. Even her *hair* looked tired. When she began her recitation, her voice was less than a whisper.

"I have four children I can't afford to feed," she said. "I can barely get out of bed in the morning. The bills are piled past the roof. My husband is serving a sentence in prison..."

Rachelle seemed to be drifting away. I wanted to shake her, to wake her up and fix her a magnificent meal.

"Look," I said. "Let's get some supplies from the back. A cucumber. Some plums. A chocolate cake. I know a place a few miles from here where we could hide—a one-room house with a gigantic porch. We could have a picnic. Move on when we felt refreshed. Afterwards, who knows? We could start a whole new, post-picnic life."

Rachelle's eyelids ruffled, drifting down like sails. Through the front windows of the Meek and Sleepy Diner I saw the police pulling into the parking lot. They'd already surrounded the Camaro and were cordoning off the diner with yellow tape, donning riot gear, and speaking through megaphones. Rachelle lifted her head a bit and yawned.

"Come on," she said.

She pulled me out of the booth, back through the kitchen's stacked pots and pans, and into the walk-in freezer. We crouched by the ventilator, Rachelle's two-fingered hand in mine. Through the vacuum-sealed door we heard boots, and snoring, and the sound of angry voices. The frozen air collected on our clothes while Rachelle and I waited, like children praying to be allowed in the house, or released from the house after a long, important lesson. With our eyes we said, "It's cold," though we tried, as best we could, to keep each other warm.

Working Out with Kafka

One day Kafka was riding his bicycle over a bridge. The tires bumped softly along the pale, uneven cobblestones. His big, twitchy ears sucked sound from the city. On the far side of the bridge, Kafka met his other self, also riding a bike.

"Well, hello!" said the other Kafka. "Fine day for a ride, don't you think?"

The first Kafka—impervious, alert, and convinced this world was prison—made no noise at all and continued on his way.

The Satisfied Cohort

I met Coleman, a co-worker of mine, in the parking garage. His patent black briefcase thunked against his leg. I had always admired the style of his suits, the crisp cut of his shirt, the super-shined footwear. I looked at my own discount dress shoes.

"How's it going?" I said.

Coleman jiggled his keys and unlocked his new silver Saab with radial tires, dual suspension, power steering and brakes, state-of-the-art Blaupunkt surround sound stereo. I unlocked my Ford Fiesta. Finally Coleman turned to me. "What's the big idea?" he asked.

"What do you mean?"

"Well, I don't know if you remember, but about three weeks ago you borrowed ten bucks from me for lunch. You remember that?"

"Oh, sure," I said.

"Well, I've been trying to be casual about it," Coleman said. "You know, waiting to see when you were going to pay me? I thought you'd repay me right away, but I've been waiting, and I guess I didn't realize what a sneaky little cheapskate you are."

"No need to get nasty," I said, "I've got it right here."

I knew what Coleman was up to, and I wasn't about to let him get away with it, so I knocked him to the asphalt. When he recovered, I pulled out a revolver and shot him. I dragged his body to a field behind the building and buried him by streetlight near the eucalyptus tree. I got in his Saab and drove to his house to pay my respects to his wife, who'd just made a tasty three-cheese lasagna, and turned out to be ferociously athletic in the sack. The next morning I went to work in one of Coleman's suits, walked into his office, and sat down at his desk. His job means an astronomical pay increase. No one seems to mind the change, and I've been doing very well ever since. I'll be promoted to management soon, and that's when I plan to start making the *really* big changes.

Woodpecker

I had just returned from the grocery store and was putting my frozen chimichangas in the freezer when I felt a sharp stabbing pain in the center of my head. I wheeled around and caught my reflection in the window—in my hair was the bright-feathered shape of a woodpecker! His little claws clutched my ear. His chiseled bill thok-thok-ed my skull.

"Fuck!"

I tried to knock him off with the chimichangas, swung, and missed. I considered calling the police.

Instead, I pulled out my wallet. I remembered I had a deluxe, triple-coil B-36 Woodpecker Obliterator tucked away in the billfold. I removed the Obliterator, and assembled it to full size, thinking *heh, heh*. I ascended the ladder, lowered myself in the cockpit, and took aim at the woodpecker—cautious, so as not to blow off my own head. The trigger squeezed easily. Sonic reverberations rocked the house. Blood spattered the cabinets. Blown-apart woodpecker bones rolled over well-scrubbed counters. What could the little bastard have wanted? I wondered, mopping up the mess. Was my head made of wood? Did he smell a tasty brain-piece in my hair?

In the bathroom I put Band-aids on my scalp and sat on the toilet, confounded. Maybe he was trying to loosen certain demons, to catch and pull free two or three wormy thoughts? Or was he a symbol, an emissary from a world made entirely of light? I lay awake that night in a sweat, twisted in the sheets, gnashing beneath a regret so deep I feared I might never emerge.

At last the sun came up. I hadn't slept at all. I got dressed and drove to the store, the gnarled walls of my brain still clogged with questions, questions, questions. I scanned the sky overhead, and saw it was swollen with birds. My car crawled the deserted streets, and I saw birds descending in dark V's to save me. The sudden sound of knocking told me someone, finally, was done for.

What Comes of Conversation

There were some mysterious circumstances surrounding the conversation. For example when I arrived and she came to the screen door in her brown, flannel robe and said, "Oh, I was sleeping."

I said, "How do you know?"

"Because I couldn't see anything," she said.

And I said, "That's no proof."

She let me into the living room where we sat on two sofas, facing each other. We talked. We had a lot of catching up to do and sat there all afternoon. Our bodies made soft sculptures in the fabric of the sofas, depressions that would remain after we'd gone into the other rooms of the house—the gleaming, clean kitchen, the hallway, the farther, bigger rooms with traps in them. Above the bookshelf, a window had been opened and what was left of the summer crawled over the sill like a dog and slunk onto the rug.

I arrived, as promised, at exactly 3:00 P.M. She lived in a house without plumbing, but there was valet parking outside, which made up for it. I gave my keys to the attendant, a college kid in a borrowed bow tie, who smiled and bowed and called me "buddy." The valet attendant's name was Pelmis Cleaver.

Her house, the house of the girl I was visiting—and it seems right to call her a girl, though often she is a woman, though mostly she is both at once, or rather first one, then the other—the house, I could tell, had been built during the Depression. It was a broken, wooden rectangle with the Depression written deep into its bones. What could we talk about, in a house like that?

"Place looks like an alms box," I said to Pelmis Cleaver.

"Sure does, buddy," Pelmis said.

But the strange thing was the conversation itself. For example, when I got inside, I noticed right away that the place had recently been cleaned. Doorknobs waxed, mint, dill and oregano sprouts carefully groomed in the windowbox, the pillows on the armchairs somewhat puffed up. I told her the place looked nice. She said "Thank you." Nothing strange about that. But when I said, "So, do you know?"

And she said, "Know what?"

And I said, "Look, it doesn't matter to me whether you know or don't. If you know, then great, hey, that's fine, but if you don't, as I might guess from the look on your face, then why are we standing here pretending?"

And she said, "Why don't you just tell me?"

I told her it was still too early, maybe if we let some time pass, to which she responded by taking off her watch and forcing it down the garbage disposal, then throwing out the house's three alarm clocks whose springs and metal parts clanged and exploded together in the garbage can like a Labor Day parade, then toppling her ancient grandfather clock from its place to the left of the bookcase which made a sound I don't even care to describe and then came back dusting her hands as if to say: There.

I said, "You think you're so clever."

She said, "Stay in the living room and wait."

When she returned from the kitchen with a bowl of roasted almonds I was sitting on the sofa.

"Almonds," she said.

I said, "Why not?"

I began to ask, Can I have a glass of water? but remembered about the plumbing.

She said, "How's work?" and I made a gesture like what is there to say about that? We searched for things to talk about. We spoke of weather and vegetables.

"Onion," I said.

She said: "Onion."

After a thoughtful pause, I asked, "Onion?"

To which she replied by saying, simply, "Onion."

Intrigued, I made an effort to heighten the discourse. "An onion is not a vegetable," I said, and my companion matched me, retorting, "A vegetable is not an onion."

We were pleased we were doing so well. Politeness poured off of our phrases like exotic waterfalls from high cliffs. I observed her as if through a seizure: brown flannel robe, eyes like singed paper, the light from her skin diffuse and intense. I told her she looked lovely. She complimented me on my new jeans, a designer brand with a little horse on the pocket. The conversation was underway. We spoke and spoke and spoke and spoke and spoke. Our talk went round like the wheel of a bicycle.

"Do you believe in God?" she asked.

I said, "If one exists, it would make perfect sense."

She said, "Has the ballad of the human heart eroded?"

"In a manner of speaking," I said.

She asked, "Do you want me to be your girlfriend?"

I didn't know what to say to that so I ate more almonds and a few moments passed.

"Why don't you answer me," she said.

I told her my mouth was full of almonds.

"You can chew, swallow, and then answer," she said.

I told her I didn't want to keep her waiting.

"You know," she said, "an almond is a symbol of fertility."

Trying to recapture the earlier, lighthearted tone of our conversation I told her an onion was a symbol of fertility too. She sighed and left the room. I stepped outside to get some air, got in the front seat of my car, turned on the air conditioning, and listened to AM radio. All the songs were about love, or about the love in someone's memory crawling to life like little animals. The songs were only people breathing. On the eaves around us, the summer light was dying. I gestured to Pelmis Cleaver.

"Looks like June going on November, eh, Pelmis?" I said.

"Sure does, buddy," the little snot said. Finally, I gave him the keys to my car and told him to keep it.

I went back inside. I found her in the medicine cabinet, rummaging around for medicine.

"What's the matter?" I asked.

"My back has been bothering me ever since I fell off that bridge," she said.

"You jumped off," I reminded her.

"Fell," she said.

"Jumped," I said.

She faced me. "I had a dream the other night," she explained. "We found a beautiful new house with a yard in the back. There were two huge rooms where we could live, a kitchen, a nice view. The house was extremely affordable. In the dream you said you didn't want to move in together because no space would be big enough for the two of us."

"That's probably what I'd say in real life," I said.

"This is real life," she said.

I wanted to argue but didn't. For a minute her face looked like it might walk away from her head.

I told her I'd given my car to Pelmis Cleaver.

She said, "Okay, I swear."

I noticed she'd changed into a shirt with the words "Do Me" written across the front. I did. We made it to the bedroom in the nick of time. I promised to build us a bridge high enough to jump off together. We cried medicine. We said we'd only talk about love because what, we asked ourselves, was more important than love? Starlight burned through the windows and the friction from our skin heated up the cold house corridors. We had chests and warm, wet places. My jeans lay on the floor where I left them, still holding the shape of my legs-- looking as if they are about to run, but running in place. And still in that same place are both of us—saying nothing, but coming and coming.

Family Scandal

A blizzard of white lines obscured the family picture. My father waved the aerials like a drowning person's arms, cursing like grandpa. The last time my father "fixed the T.V." he put his foot through the screen. Then for two months we had no T.V.

I went to my room and listened to the radio. The DJ has a voice like my friend whose father is a telephone repairman. My friend's father looks like mine, except for the tool belt and the toothpick in his teeth. Once he came to our house to fix the telephone, which hadn't worked in two months. Mother thought he was her husband in a tool belt and accidentally embraced him. Unfortunately, my father walked in just then. He put his foot through the screen door, then moved out. We didn't talk to him for two months because the telephone was broken.

Alone in his miserable hotel, my father began to write songs. He wrote "Static in My Heart" and "Miscommunication." They were instant Top 40 hits. The DJ with my friend's voice played them every night, fighting bad reception. In low, mellifluous tones he dedicated the songs to me. I listened, wishing my mother would come up to talk.

Instead I called my friend. (His father had since fixed the telephone). My friend came by to watch T.V. I told him my grandpa was an actor in the early days of television. "A family scandal cost him his job," I said. "He had to go back to working in radio."

My mother was on the back porch singing "Static in My Heart."

"Wow," said my friend in his deep, sweet voice. "How embarrassing."

The Reason We Were So Afraid

The reason we were so afraid was that Eddie and me were just sitting there on our green sofa, watching Tatie crawl around in her white diapers, making seven-month-old faces, and we were feeling really proud and cozy when Tatie looked us in the eyes and said, "Why not pick me up for a bit?"

Naturally, we thought we'd imagined it. She didn't say anything for a while, just glared at us and gurgled, but over the next hour she said, "You betcha," "Get off of my cloud," and "Please pass the milk."

We picked her up and carried her around, then wrapped her in some warmer blankets. When we gave her Gerber's mashed peas she said, "Just wait till I get my teeth." We tried to pretend like nothing was different and said, "Gitchy gitchy goo" while tickling her little chin. She said, "Stop that."

Well, we were totally frantic by then so we stuffed her in the Pocahontas pajamas and rushed to the clinic. The doctor told us the baby was perfectly healthy and there was no sign of anything amiss. He put a stethoscope on Tatie's chest and she said, "Aaah, that thing is freezing!" The doctor muttered, "Perfectly healthy," and put Tatie's pajamas back on. Tatie picked at the plastic Pocahontas, then said in an exasperated tone, "Can we go?"

When we got back from the clinic we consulted our Dr. Spock book. Dr. Spock told us the child needs to be surrounded by the right child environment.

So we rushed to Toys "R" Us and charged one hundred dollars worth of Fisher Price toys on our MasterCard, then came home and set up the bouncing balls and the rubber xylophones and the big fuzzy cuddlers that burped and said I love you but Tatie turned to us with a totally blank expression and said, "A person needs space if they're to grow up healthy and integrated in this world beset by chaos and deep suffering."

Well, Eddie and me just about burst out into tears right then. Maybe we did something wrong? we said. I rushed to the bookshelf and looked through our baby books. B.F. Skinner said sometimes the child assimilates the behavior and speech of the parents.

So Eddie and me decided to only talk baby talk, even to each other. "Would choo like a little din-din?" I said to Eddie. "Hoo-way!" he cheered and clapped his hands.

The baby just rolled her eyes and said, "Please."

We bought manuals and instruction tapes. We consulted experts. We tried hypnotism, positive reinforcement, reverse psychology, passive-aggressive parenting, and clowns. We filled whole rooms with Legos and Lincoln Logs, but the baby liked Mussorgsky and the paintings of Francis Bacon.

On her first birthday, we opened the door to Tatie's nursery and found her propped up in bed reading Heidegger. She was wearing a black turtleneck and working her way through a pack of French cigarettes. "Don't you want to do something to celebrate your birthday?" we asked her hopefully, but Tatie just said, "What's the use?" and threw the book aside. Then she buried her head in her hands and whispered, "Life is so short."

Well, Eddie and me couldn't help but agree.

Old House

It seemed so simple in the middle of the night to walk outside the house again, calling your name.

The house and I are similar. It leans with peeling paint, the porch old, uneven. The grass is wet where I walk in sandals and the moon dips down whenever I freeze, my face against the glass.

I had learned to throw my voice and hoped that you would catch it. I thought the house would absorb what I could not hold. I felt the map of the house unfold in my pocket, while the shadow I crouched in fit me, like a coat I'd lost, then recovered, its empty sleeve still drifting.

I knock every night, though I know the house is empty, so it's emptiness I'm knocking on and emptiness that answers. The rooms all swept, the bed raffled off, the walls smooth where my gaze falls through the opened window.

I stand outside and sympathize.

I know how lonely the house is when there is no one to live there.

Answering Machine

Beep!

Hello. If this is the home of Tom Magrath, I'm calling about the room for rent. If it's still available, I'd be interested in talking to you and perhaps arranging a time to come see it. My name is Lester Kandinsky and I can be reached evenings at 671-5210. Thanks.

Beep!

Morning, sorryass. You are *supposed to be home.* We had some, uh, things to attend to today, if I remember correctly. Contact me as soon as you get this message.

Beep!

Hi, it's me. I'm at the office now, as you probably could guess. It's about 9:30 and I'll be very impressed if you're not answering the phone because you're actually out of bed and out of the apartment. Most grown-ups are by this time, you know. But chances are you're not out of bed and out of the apartment but still under the covers, lying there not answering this call. If that's the case, I give you exactly three seconds to pick up the receiver. ....
Okay then, the reason I'm calling is that I can't remember if we made plans for today. Did we make some? I can't meet you for lunch because I've got my session. Tonight I'm working late, but I should be able to come over about 7:00. Or maybe you could come to my place, for a change. Gee, what a novel idea. Call me

at work today and we'll arrange something. Either way, I'll order some take-out and pick it up on the way home. Chinese? Bye.

Beep!

Hey, Tom, Phillip. Cards tonight, right? Call me.

Beep!

Tom, this is Kevin. Look, I know I already call you way too much, and I know it's a little early in the morning for my confessions of existential confusion and self-loathing, but I have to talk to somebody, man. I don't know what it is. I can't work. I can't concentrate on anything for more than five seconds. I'm lost. I can't bear to be around Jessica. She's like a stranger to me nowadays, a rustling past of clothes. I had to make the excuse of going to the store just to get out of the apartment for a minute, just to make this goddamn phone call. Look, Tom, I know you're sick of hearing about it, but I really need to see you tonight. I have to try to talk out my mind. You're a rock to me sometimes, man, a life raft. Can I come over? Call me. I have to go buy milk.

Beep!

Hi, Tom, it's Mom. Aunt Flora called me *again* this morning to ask if we were coming to the reunion or not and I told her that I just didn't know yet because you *still* hadn't told me about next weekend and whether or not you'd be able to go. I'm waiting for your answer! Anyway, I'm here as usual, holding the household together—doing laundry and watching Sally Jessy Raphael. There's a guest panel of cross-dressing lesbians squaring off against Hamburg's Neo-Nazi faction. What will they think of next! Anyway, I love you and call me back when you get home. Bye!

Beep!

Hi, it's Mom again. I just talked to Aunt Flora on the phone and she says there's going to be an Oompah band at the reunion! Doesn't that sound like fun? Anyway, she was pressing me for an answer so

I told her we'd definitely be there and that we'd bring all the paper plates and napkins. Don't you want to take some time off and drive up and eat some barbecue and play softball with the kids? You used to love to go when you were younger. You should really try to come, Tom. You know, Herbert and Wilameena aren't going to be around much longer and neither are Uncle Noel and Chuggs. You'll be sorry that you didn't spend more time with them after they're gone. Family is important, Thomas—it's time for you to realize that. Anyway, it sounds like it's going to be great and I really, really want to go. But if you can't make it, then I guess I won't go either. I'll just stay home. You know, I really don't understand what you do with your time, honey. Over thirty and don't even have a proper career yet? I try not to worry, but it's hard. The least you could do is set my mind at ease by doing something for me every once in a while. Anyway, I don't want to pressure you, sweetie. If you can't come, I understand. Anyway, I'll call again later when Dad comes home. Do you want to come over for dinner tonight? I'm going to make your favorite: green bean casserole! Love you.

Beep!

Tom, it's Jessica. When I got home last night, I didn't take a shower because I wanted to keep your smell on my body. Kevin didn't even notice, or if he did, he didn't say anything. I've been thinking about you all morning, Tom. My muscles ache from you. Your smell is all over my hands and belly. I'm whispering because Kevin's in the next room and I don't want him to hear, though it's not like he'd care anyway. I don't even care if he knows. All I want is to fuck you. Can I see you tonight? I go crazy thinking about your neck. I'm sweating between my legs right now. Please come over tonight and get me. Kevin is going out with Casey for beers at 8:00. Don't say you can't come. I'll be home all night. I'll be waiting for you in my nightshirt with nothing underneath. I can't wait to have your dick in my mouth.

Beep!

Uh, hi, I hope this is the right number... If it is... I'm calling about the room for rent... and I, uh, I really hope it's not taken because

I think Hillcrest is a pretty great area and I really need a place to live and it's like close to my school so that would be convenient if I could, y'know, live there. Uh... well... it sounds like you're not home so I guess I'll just leave a number and maybe you could call me back, huh? Or maybe I should try to call you again later? Well, I'll just leave my number anyway. Okay, so the number at my mom's house is 671–2515 and my name is Caleb. That's Caleb, 671–25... 15. I'll be home tonight after nine when I finish basketball practice and you can call me then. I really, really want my own place and yours sounds really great so don't give it to anybody else, okay? Okay... bye.

Beep!

Hi, Tom, it's Ann again. I'm still at the office but I'm just about to leave for lunch. I thought you might be home by now, but *obviously* not. Why is it that you never seem to be home when I call? Sometimes I feel like the only time I get to really talk to you is on this answering machine. Sometimes it seems like I've got an obsessive-compulsive relationship with the telephone. But I think it's not the instrument so much as an obsession with communication. That's healthy, right? Anyway, you know why communication is so important to me? Do you? I'll tell you. It's because we live in an age where we are increasingly estranged from each other and the only way to bridge the gap is to try even harder. You know? I've talked to my therapist a lot about this and he says it's a natural, healthy, human impulse. Nothing wrong with it at all. Anyway, I'm going to talk with him some more about it today. I'm going to my session in thirty minutes, after I grab some lunch at Soup Exchange. Call me at the office this afternoon! Bye.

Beep!

Hello, Mr. Magrath, this is Ed Carpenter calling from Aceland Firearms and Accessories. I'm just giving you a call to let you know that your special order Winchester arrived today and you can come down any time and pick it up as long as you bring along your license and registered papers and so forth. We're open until six every day. See you soon.

Beep!

Hey, Tom, this is Casey. It's about 2:30 and I'm just calling to see if you want to go out with Kevin and me tonight for beers at The Alibi. You know, I.... uh... I'm really worried about that guy. He just hasn't seemed like himself lately. I was hoping you could come along and help talk some sense into him. I can't remember if you play cards on Tuesday or Wednesday. Anyway, if you're free tonight, it'd be great to have you there and it would give you the chance to get away from Ann for an evening. Call me back if you want to come. See ya.

Beep!

Hello? Tom? This is your conscience, motherfucker. Still no word from you, man. I've been available all day. I was thinking that maybe, just maybe, you might get up the nerve to discuss our "options." You know where I am.

Beep!

Hello, this telephone message is for Mr. Tom Magrath and it concerns his advertisement in Sunday's paper for a room to let. My name is Harold LeSourd and I am an accounts representative with Hewlitt-Packard currently living in the downtown area and seeking a change of living location. If it's feasible for you, Mr. Magrath, please contact me at one of the following numbers and times: 671–8351 before noon. 615–5123 before 5:00 o'clock in the evening. You can also call me at home at 608–5361; I am usually only there in the late evenings but you can also leave a message there with my message service. I hope to be hearing from you sometime very soon.

Beep!

Yeah, I called last week about the apartment and you never called me back. This is Buzz, remember, the drummer for Fetid Stench? Anyway, I got kicked out of my place and I really need a place to practice so call me back this time, alright?

Beep!

It's Kevin. I'm suffocating on the sound of my breathing. Oh, Tom. My world is so small I could fly to pieces at any moment. What do I care? I have to be secretive. I'm only calling because Jessica went out for a walk. I can't explain to her. I can't explain to anyone. People are like machines, Tom. They overload and go haywire. I'm supposed to meet Casey tonight. I can't bear it. He's a liar and a backstabber and he wants to fuck my girlfriend. What do I care? Have you ever suspected Ann of fucking her shrink, Tom? Have you ever asked her? Are you a gambling man? You seem to understand these matters. You are a strong, important man.

Beep!

Tom, this is Rick. I heard from the other guys that cards are on for tonight at your place at seven. You got beer, I hope? See you at seven.

Beep!

Tom, it's Jessica. I told Kevin I was going for a walk so I could come outside and call you from the pay phone. I have my hand in my sweatpants, I'm touching myself and picturing your mouth. Its snarls and long tunnels. I'm picturing the whole of you as a cock inside me, my mouth crammed full of you. Bent over chairs, tables. I'll leave the door unlocked after eight.

Beep!

Hi... I'm angry. It's Ann. We're going over to my place tonight and that's all there is to it. I'm sorry I'm yelling, I guess I'm a little upset with you. Well, I guess this is just projected anger at this very moment but, I don't know, in general, I guess, it springs from the dysfunctional elements of our relationship. I just got back from my session, Tom, where my therapist made me talk about your self-proclaimed "independence." He told me that it's partially a front that enables you to maintain control in the relationship. Like the way you always make us sleep at your apartment because you say you can't sleep well at my place because it's not your own "space," and you know I'm making the finger quotations. My therapist said I should demand that we sleep at my place sometimes, that I should insist on egalitarian spatial and psychic arrangements. Those were his exact words. It's a big pain for me to always have to come over there after work and then I have to go back to my place to get dressed because that's where all my clothes are because you won't let me keep any clothes in your closet. Not even one friggin T-shirt. Why do you do that? It's really weird. I told my therapist about it and he said you had a barrier. One article of clothing is not going to compromise your independence, Tom. Can't I just keep one change of clothes? How about a sock? So even on my day off I could go out without having to drive all the way back to my place? It's really not that big a deal. I don't know... Maybe you should think about seeing someone, Tom. I mean it. Therapy has helped a lot of people and it doesn't mean you're compromising yourself if you go. Not everyone can solve their own problems, you know. It doesn't mean you're weak. All you have to do is sit on the couch and say whatever comes into your head. How can that be threatening? You don't even have to say anything if you don't want to. When I first started going I was really skeptical and resistant but I found out pretty soon that my skepticism stemmed from my fear of letting other people in. I had a wall, Tom. I'd been carrying it around with...

Beep!

Oops! Got cut off. Anyway, I'd been carrying my wall around for a long time and since I've been in therapy I've discovered that everyone has their own walls. You too, sweetie. If you could for just one minute stop being so steely and self-sufficient all the time you might find that other people have a lot to offer. Do you know what I mean? Anyway, well... whatever. So... do you want me to come over tonight or what?

Beep!

Hello, Tom, this is Dean Jakobson calling. I just wanted to remind you that, according to my calendar, today is the first of the month and I'll be by to collect the rent this evening between 7:00 and 8:00. I don't know if you've found someone to fill the vacated room yet, but if you haven't, I'm afraid I'll have to ask you for the full rent now and you can have the new tenant reimburse you for their half when you get that sorted out. It's an unpleasant situation, but you do have a lease to fulfill and, anyway, I'm sure that by now you've picked out a fine roommate. You've certainly had plenty of time! At any rate, I'll see you this evening between 7:00 and 8:00. Goodbye.

Beep!

Hi! It's Mom! Just calling again to check in and also to say that I forgot to say earlier that I finished your laundry and I can drive it over tonight, if you want, and then, if you want, I can bring you back for dinner and Dad can drive you home in the Vanogan later. I starched your good dress shirts like you wanted and I used fabric softener on all the whites so they're nice and fluffy. You should really come for dinner, honey. Rex misses you. And your father would like to see you too... Tell him, Doug. .... Hey son, you know how I hate talking to these machines. Why don't you come on over for dinner and pay us a little visit? Well, here's your mother. .... Hi! It's me again! Well, I guess I'll see you when I come over with your laundry. I hope you'll come for dinner. Green bean casserole! Mm mm good! Well, see you in a bit!

Beep!

Hey, fucker. Have you been thinking about what you're going to do? Have you weighed the pozzzzibilteeeees? You know, there's an easy way out of every situation. But you don't want to, uh... how shall we say... jump the gun? You wouldn't want to... blow it. You wouldn't want that now, would you?

Beep!

Hey, Tom, Phillip again. Did Rick leave a message on your machine? I tried to call him about 4:30 to let him know that we were on for tonight, but couldn't get hold of him. I left a message on Dave's machine telling him to call Rick and tell him if he got the chance. Otherwise, everybody else knows. Hey, your psychotic girlfriend isn't going to be there, is she? I don't know how you cope with her, man. I would have cracked under that pressure long ago. I would have lost it. Anyway, we're all meeting at The Alibi at six for some beforehand beers. Meet us there?

Beep!

Hi, Tom, this is Casey. Just calling to see if you were in yet and what your plans were. Have you heard from Kevin lately? I made a plan with him earlier in the week for tonight but I haven't been able to reach him. Then again, talking to him at all lately has kinda been like talking to the air. Oh yeah, what's happening with your extra room? Did you find a renter yet? It's a bitch trying to find a roommate. There's a lot of weirdos out there that can make life impossible, if you know what I mean. Anyway, good luck. See you at The Alibi if you decide to come.

Beep!

Tom, Where are you? I haven't gone home yet. I've been walking around all day with your mouth in my mind. I have to see you now. I'm going to climb in your window and wait in your bed. My cunt is a cave to swallow you. I'll be there and wait there for you.

Beep!

Christ, Tom, where are you? It's 6:30 and you aren't home yet? All of us are here at The Alibi. Maybe you're just not picking up the phone? You're probably just sitting there, you bastard, listening to your machine, laughing to yourself. You're a weird guy, Tom. Sometimes I get the feeling that you're kind of hanging back in yourself and judging everyone, keeping a bird's-eye view of the situation. You always got that kinda superior smile on your face. Is that why you look that way? Anyway, me and the guys are coming over at 7:00 for the game ready or not and if you're not there we're gonna bust in the door. If you get this message in the next twenty minutes, come to The Alibi.

Beep!

Tom. Tom. Tom, it's me. It's me, Kevin. Why don't you answer? I know you are there as much or more than me. I mean, sometimes I'm sure I'm here because I know the sound of my own voice. I mean, this is my voice you're hearing, isn't it? I mean, how much can you trust this machine? It's everything. Well, I'm going to The Alibi to get drunk. I have a bad feeling, Tom. I have the feeling something terrible is going to happen. Maybe I should come to see you first. I know, I know you can help me...

Beep!

Hi, honey. Where are you? Listen, I'm sorry about my tirade earlier, I was just a little worked up after the session. Sometimes I just have to signal the voice in my brain to stop talking in order not to go crazy! Anyway, I'll be finished with work in about forty-five minutes and then I'll get take-out Chinese and come on over. If you're not there by then, I'll let myself in with my key and wait for you. We'll talk about everything later tonight. Something's got to give sooner or later. If you're still out and call to check your messages, leave a message for me letting me know when you'll be there. I love you, honey. Bye.

Beep!

Hey, you there? Anybody home? .... Huh? .... Yeah, that's what I thought. Okay, you ready, motherfucker?

Letter from One Half of Myself to the Other

Dear friend. All this echo comes back to you. My days are very long. I've been spending some time in the library, maybe too much. For breakfast I eat grapes and cheese. For lunch, I generally drink about fifteen glasses of water. It's essential to stay well hydrated, don't you think? In the afternoons I'm squeezed by boredom, and pace the house, scrubbing spots in the carpet with my thumb. If I had a television, I'd watch golf, or a talk show about sisters who marry their own adopted sisters—but I don't have a television. Nights I go to the grocery store. Everyone there speaks in code. It's decipherable, but I worry, because the messages don't seem deep enough, or they are so deep that they upend the world, embody contradiction, and spiral into nothing. But enough about me. How are you? I imagine that you're working hard, or taking out the garbage. Listen. Let me ask you something. Can't we pretend to be together for a minute? Like we're actually part of the same enterprise? I need you to feel whole again. I miss your neck muscles, and have thought often of your blue, hand-woven sombrero.

The Unfortunate Poker Game

I lost it all in the poker game—buttons, billfold, cuff links, boots, velvet fedora, grandmother's china, the deed to my house, and a few fancy lamps. I left in my socks in the rain. At home I filled a canteen with water, got some cash from the mattress, took a last look around, then stumbled into the world: a drifter in a desolate desertscape.

That's when I decided to get a covered wagon. A frontiersman like me needed one, I figured. A canvas house nailed to a sturdy wood skeleton, a freewheeling rustic mobile abode.

I went to the mall where they'd just opened a new Wagons and Things. Bright lights flooded stacks of huge wooden wheels; rumble seats were heaped by the register. A salesman in a flashy cowboy hat approached. His name tag said "My Future." In his husky voice My Future swore he could see me in this year's model, just in, and could shave a good portion off the sticker price since he could tell I was a guy who knew his wagons.

"Or how about a hackney?" he said. "We got horses in the outlet."

"No thanks," I said. "Just the covered."

Money changed hands, My Future smiled, and I heeya-ed out of the parking lot. This world is a loop of incongruities, I thought. Soon I was rambling over prairie, singing high lonesome tunes. I felt good with my wagon. It was somewhere to be. Years elapsed beneath moon and stars, clattering past cacti in my covered home.

One day—when the sun was spilling overhead and my mind was calm and clear—I was overtaken by a band of outlaws. Their well-polished pistols caught light in the late afternoon. "Geddown," they barked. I knew them from the poker game: bristly black beards, eyes glinting over red bandanas. They took my last money, the clothes off my back, and climbed in the wagon.

"My crutch," I said.

The last thing I saw was the wagon weaving toward the skyline, my pants flown behind like a flag. Since that day, I have not stopped walking; naked as the day I was born. My feet are the texture of dirt, but my song—half-confused and tuneless—still threads the way. "I have measured my stakes and played," it goes, "and nothing left to lose. Before me is the open road, not a sign or a symbol between us."

The Suicide

Imagine a kitchen with all the lights on, a curtain in the window rearranged by wind, a knife going into the heart. In your hands, on the wooden tabletop, the letter is unfolded. Your hands are absolutely still, but also full of fury since emptiness is a mountain we must slash down every minute while inside us there's another mountain hatching. The letter takes hold of its lie. Its small, brittle lines double as instructions to indicate pitch, latitude, and what ways to properly ventilate the chest. Repetition finds us endlessly leaving. Autumn returns as the mother of fear. Carefully, rethink each and every year, then touch the page with disintegrating fingers so the skeleton of your old self is seen one last time, the way a leaf falling tells its life to the tree.

Gift Exchange

True Confessions of the Bat-Fonz

I was about to throw myself through a plate-glass window when the telephone rang. I answered saying, "Hi. No one's home," and hung up.

Two minutes later it rang again. This time I said, "Foo-whin-yaa-nee," annunciating clearly so they'd understand, then slammed down the receiver.

The morning had not begun auspiciously. Several of my teeth had fallen down the drain. Hair kept coming out in fistfuls. When I opened the blinds to look outside, I saw the neighbors' houses had been blown up by explosives. All the local dogs were dead. In the pit of my stomach I had a terrible feeling that I was somehow responsible.

The blinds unsheathed a splendorous, sunny day. "At least the weather's holding," I sighed, and wept a few tears of joy. Then I snorted. Soon, I was laughing uncontrollably. The morning passed in this way, until the phone rang again, and I grabbed it with both hands.

On the other end someone said, "We are calling to inform you that the circumstances leading to the creation of your opulently volatile emotional nature and the dangerously complex landscape of your mind might bear a methodical, reasoned examination at this time if you ever wish to achieve any sense of success or social stability in this feeble, transient life."

"I'm sorry," I replied coolly, "but I don't accept sales calls. Can you please take me off your list?"

I hung up and slunk into the kitchen, greatly perturbed. What kind of fool did they take me for? Soon I'd prepared an elaborate breakfast: Orange juice, eggs, fruit salad, grits, biscuits and gravy, bacon, a couple of pancakes, and six cups of coffee. I ate, and felt much better. The kingdom of heaven was snaking through my veins, in fact. Music covered the earth. I changed into a pair of shorts, grabbed a lawn chair, and dashed outside to get myself a tan.

Same Game

Every day at the bus stop I see this little kid, about eight years old, hooded sweatshirt and white Nikes, bouncing a blue racquetball against the stippled asphalt.

"Catch," she said yesterday, and threw the ball in my direction.

Its rubber surface felt strange in my fingers, like a piece of fruit I didn't know the name of. It was still pretty early in the morning, and a heavy cloud cover hung low on the buildings. Everything looked like a shadow of itself. I'd seen this kid the day before, and the day before that, and she never seemed to be going anywhere, not school or camp or someone's house. She scared me. Her face was like a slate where you could scribble new expressions.

Finally, she said, "You look sad. Where are you going?"

"To work," I told her. "Everyday I take the bus, same time. See my briefcase? It's an adult thing. When you grow up, you'll see. It's not sad. You ride the bus, work, come home at night. Like that." I tossed the ball back. "You?" I asked. "Where're you going?"

The built-in reflector on the girl's sneaker gleamed. She said, "I'm going to be brave in ways you won't recognize." Then she pocketed her racquetball and ran away from me.

I'd Heard She Had a Deconstructive Personality

Then saw her on the sidewalk. A crash course. A kiss. In the bus. On the floor. With a book, legs set for the span of attention. Mind filling like a zeppelin. The alley. The abstract. Her feet the root of a word. Her head an eraser, no shading or shadow. I saw her at the bus stop. Whole body a tympanic drum brushed by a broom. Whole body a panda, unmotorized Victrola, miserable rat hole. Here and then here. Poppies exploding, smoke. I called her—got to know her. Her secret self an igloo, covered with silly string. We talked until memory milked out all her mistakes. On the telephone. In an airplane. My fingers flashed in. Her fingers hang to dry on the back of a battleship, but her legs have touched the earth where the dirt makes its list of the powerless and blessed. She washed the make-up from her face for good. I asked her near me. She said, "Rest."

My Nap

There was a day last week when I was feeling like a colossal loser. I was doing nothing right and no one liked me. I went straight home and got into bed. I decided to pretend that I was dead. For three hours I pretended. I don't remember much of it. I have a vague recollection of my friend Alex knocking on the door.

"Come in," I said. He opened the door and asked what I was doing.

"Don't talk to me," I said, "I'm dead."

Alex went to my refrigerator to look for beer. "Is this the afterlife?" I said. "Are those gleaming fixtures the features of angels?" Alex asked where the bottle opener was. I floated off the bed in my superbody, addressing the undulant chromosphere. "This is amazing," I whispered.

Alex took a seat by the window, watching me. "What are you *doing*?" he asked. I spliced through the ceiling and dissolved into a table. Once there I ate an orange and wrote a postcard to the president. The postcard read: "Dear Mr. President, I am dead and I can assure you that the otherworld compares quite favorably to this one. Life is not Life. Please destroy everything so we can all be happy." I told Alex to rush to the post office and mail the postcard immediately. He sighed and went in my kitchen to make himself a sandwich.

When three hours had elapsed I opened my eyes to see Alex picking breadcrumbs from the plate. I got off the bed: my spine jangled like the tines of a rake, metal gurgled in my throat. "What happened?" I asked. Alex shrugged. I blinked. I staggered to the door and opened it on an orange hallway waiting, searing poly-voiced orchestras, flashes of applause. I was demolished, reissued, clean as a white-hot jewel. I felt altogether better and well rested.

Compliments

I leave a letter for Melissa on the dresser by the bed. Red roses in a cut-glass vase. The letter reads, My dearest darling of whom there is no darling dearer.

In a fit of excitement, I fall back to sleep. I dream Melissa is standing over me, shining knife in hand. When I wake up she is cooking me breakfast: toast browns on a paper towel, the orange juice decanted to little cups. Her smile cannot be quantified in terms of radiance. I ask her if she read the letter. "Fifteen times," she says. She slices the sausages steady and thin.

"You are the most wonderful," she tells me.

"No, you," I say.

"No, *you.*"

We dress in the dim light of the bedroom. Half in shadow, we blink and squint. Her body seems the blueprint of perfection. Stilt-like roots, dense thickets growing along tidal shores. I see her looking at my torso, backlit from the light in the kitchen. "In silhouette like that," she says, "you almost look like Charles Atlas."

"Thanks!" I say.

We snap on straps and buttons. *You look so good in that dress. That shirt becomes you.*

Melissa flicks on a lamp.

"To me you are a spiny sculpin treading the murky lagoon," she says.

"Thanks!" I say.

In the living room I notice she has set out some gifts for me: An elegant bronze pipe stand, an accompanying tobacco box inlaid with beautiful tile, a bronze ashtray with my initials in calligraphy on the bottom.

"I carved them myself," she tells me.

"You shouldn't have!"

We admire the box's glittering paraphernalia. Melissa picks up the pipe-cleaning blade in a deliberate way. Her creativity has inspired me. I rush out to the backyard and begin to build a birdhouse. I use the Black and Decker power-saw to halve standard sheets of plywood. The sound of the saw thrills me.

The birdhouse is finished in forty-five minutes. I hang it from the cedar by the fence, adorned with green tassel and three hummingbird feeders. Melissa is overjoyed.

"The birds will be so happy!" she says.

There are those unfortunates who only fantasize about ideal love. Melissa and I sit on the porch swing, hands interlaced, nails making deep indentations at the wrist. We pity the unfortunates.

"Who could be as good a swimmer?" I ask.

"Who a finer teller of stories?" she retorts.

"Did I tell you the one about the time my family picked up a hitchhiking nun?"

"Yes," she says.

We look out on the garden, smiling. Radish greens and lettuce tips peek up from the earth. In the gentle rocking of the porch swing, our hearts glare and glow. Most sweetest etcetera most darling etcetera most special etcetera etcetera.

We stroll through the park in tan slacks and visors. The sun covers us like a quilt. We collect hibiscus and look for the rare anhydrous creeping philodendron. Leaves curl over to offer shade while birds themselves address us. Melissa walks ahead a little and I reach down, pick up a large stone, and cock my arm to a pitcher's arc, taking steady aim. Melissa turns around.

"Look what I found!" I say suddenly, showing her the stone.

"Pretty!" she says.

Melissa goes to the store and I am in despair. How long will she be gone? Fifteen minutes? Thirty? I write her a twelve page letter. It begins:

> The hour is black. There is nothing but desolation. I await your return with a body wound like a rubberband. My memory is plastered with posters of you. I could do some things...

Immediately I mail the letter to the supermarket. I set up an easel in the drawing room, then gather up canvasses, paints, camel-hair brushes. I want to paint her likeness before her face fades from memory. I have only begun when she returns from the store.

"What's that?" she asks.

"It's a portrait of you!"

"My nose isn't that long."

"Yes it is... sure it is."

"Well," she says wisely, "I guess beauty is in the eye of the beholder."

We laugh: tickle tickle.

She begins to cook dinner, coming in every once in a while to check the painting. She gestures at the canvas with a serving spoon.

"Why do I have a cleft palate?"

"Just a little artistic license," I say.

She marvels at my skill and invention. She turns up the heat in the oven.

Melissa's cooking is beyond me: souffles and venison, liver pate, rice with raisins. We sit down to dinner and darken the room.

"How do you get these green beans so tender?" I ask. "These potatoes are perfection itself!"

I bring her fifty bouquets of flowers. "Take them!" I say.

She demands to know where the irises are. I open up the bureau and withdraw a full-sized reproduction of an ancient Mexican statue, the imposing form of Aztec warrior Polexamaquaatl, mouth crammed with long-stemmed irises.

"Oh, sweetie!"

We kiss: tickle tickle.

"More wine?" I ask and fill her glass. She says, "No thanks" and I continue to pour. The wine flows over the glass, onto the table, and splashes on the carpet. We wade around in it ankle deep.

"Fine vintage," I say.

"A '62," she informs me.

After dinner we move to the bedroom for a brandy. In the dim, romantic light we blink and squint. She empties something from a blue vial into my brandy glass; I slip a bludgeon beneath the mattress. Love is the quiet moments like these, the precious hours we recognize our heart's true treasure. It is always that I am for her and she is for me. Candles flicker our faces to half-shadow.

"You look beautiful," she tells me.

"You're nothing to shake a stick at either," I say.

When I lean over so our lips might touch, I tell her, earnestly: "I would never shake a stick at you, Melissa... not in this light..."

The Great Grandson of J. Alfred Prufrock

You get home from work, exhausted. You hate your job: assembling plastic flip-down visors in a car factory. You've stolen a pair for your '81 Corolla, but the brakes are still shot, and you can't save the money to fix them. As a result, you nearly mowed down a Girl Scout at the crosswalk this morning. Tell yourself it's all right. Come in and collapse on the couch. The yellow light of the low-rent room depresses you; it gnaws your thoroughly well-chewed self-worth. Put your feet up. Your 13-year-old daughter should be home from school by now, but she's in a neighbor's basement, begging some boy to do her. Try to relax and rest easy. Sort through the day's mail. The telephone bill is 120 dollars; weird surcharges, extra connection fees. You have $208 in the bank. Nothing to worry about. Sure, tension has knotted your neck, and anxiety makes it impossible to sit still but you jump up anyway because you are sure someone's outside—there have been break-ins in the neighborhood. You stand in the living room, look through the blinds, and the whole existential predicament fries in your mind like an egg. Someone *is* outside. There's a knock at the door. You open it and a woman enters in white robes, bright red bindi in the center of her forehead. She hands over a small cotton pouch, studded with miniature pearls, which you open at once and just then your soul shoots from your body like a speeding train and you go gazing at the cosmos' frivolous bric-a-brac with a huge translucent face. Shortly afterward, you'll be dead for good. So you see, it's no big deal, really. Everything's totally cool.

The Last Trick I Learned

Like every time before that last one we came up out of our lives and kicked at the orange dirt and cups, walked across the tramped-down streamers and continued, light-footed, through the circus ground. We heard carousel music and met each other in the hall of mirrors saying, Love lasts forever. At the time we thought our hearts were whole. I had said and she had said. The midway unfolded thick as a carpet before us, all the lights of the city stretched there and we could imagine no end. We thought: Columbus was wrong, the earth *is* flat. Meanwhile, candy was being cooked in little ovens, children laughed themselves breathless, two men washed the coats of prize dogs. I changed a dollar. She watched, a gaze that rang in the smashed evening. I held a burnt sparkler and swore to remember her look—the look of all that is never undone, the look of words we won't ever unsay.

Someone swallowed swords. "I'll just be a minute," she said, and left to buy popcorn. I sat down on the metal stair and put my head in my hands. I began to think about it all, that cord that pulls us along, the tricks we'd taught ourselves, the acrobatic shadow dance. It was summer when we started, eight years ago. The first night we slept together we pulled the mattress on the narrow balcony of her sixth floor apartment. We joked about a passion so fierce it would send us tumbling over the ledge. Remembering it, I did not laugh. She wasn't back yet. I went looking for the popcorn stall. A minute is a long time.

I pulled my feet past men shouting Guess Your Weight! I found her watching clowns: one atop a giant unicycle teetered, arms a-flail. The crowd gasped as he plummeted to a trampoline the size of a button. We applauded and ate popcorn. Happiness, we knew, was a window through which one walks, but is not transparent. Our feet ached and our breath came jagged. We passed the shooting gallery and the coin toss. Impresarios coaxed us. We went to the booth of all the futures we'd tried to dream but couldn't. We were addicted.

We lay in a field behind the blazing big top. Weeds sprouted up through our hair and crickets sidled past us. The night moved away, then turned inside itself, and I kissed her in my memory. At the top of the Ferris wheel some kids swung their stopped car. "We can't go on like this forever," she said. I felt the curve of the earth beneath my back. When an hour had passed, she reached for my hand but I pulled it away. "Sometimes the something that you need to do is nothing," I said.

Back in the swirling midway monkeys played piano and we danced, wrapped in each other's clothes. Our dumb world was an apple dipped in caramel, prizes. We pulled our bodies apart. This is how I want to remember it. A piñata was being beaten with sticks and when it burst, small notes fluttered to the ground. They read: Grace is the love that will not let you go. They read: In case of emergency, read this piece of paper. We laughed. Everything was meaningless. I wanted so much to run off and join the circus, to learn to walk a tightrope but I knew even there I would be careless and fall. The look she wore then was asking, it was halfway between two places and the smile hung on her face as if by a hinge. "Come closer," I said, and the hinge swung open.

86 Things That Happened Between 2:35 and 2:38 While I Was Lying on My Bed Trying to Take a Nap

1) At 2:35 I lay down on my bed to take a quick nap. 2) The minute my head hit the pillow I started thinking about "achievement."

3) Things were not right. The disorderliness of my one-room, sparely furnished, low-rent apartment distracted me. 4) A large, black fly buzzed over the bed, then vibrated against the window screen.

5) The Buddhists say everything exists inside the mind but that's ridiculous because I knew for a fact that the fly, which at that moment was buzzing around the room—going *zzzt* to the desk, *zzzt* to the kitchen counter, *zzzt* to the ceiling above me-- was *not* in my mind. My mind might have been quiet, calm, and peaceful if not for the goddamn buzzing.

6) I sniffled some against the pillow and shut my eyes. Sometimes life exhausts me. Also, I was unemployed, and getting older. Why else a nap at 2:35 on a Tuesday afternoon? 7) My father, I felt fairly certain, would not be proud.

8) The fly settled on an old bowl of cereal. 9) I counted One Mississippi. 10) I looked at the window, scanned my desktop, glanced at the stereo until finally, in the corner of the room on the ceiling, I saw it: hairy as Kong and big as a 747.

10) The fly nose-dove from the ceiling, reconnoitering over my shoulders with a roar. 11) I turned on my side, annoyed-- All I wanted was a nap. Are the simplest things most difficult to achieve? 12) I shifted the quilt, sniffing a rivulet of mucus.

13) Weird sounds were coming through the wall. Like every night Walter was next door, hobbling to his toaster oven. He's old, and in worse shape even than me. 14) I followed the fly's course with my eyes and watched it frizzle in circles near the refrigerator. 15) I imagined the words "Delta Airlines" written on its side. 16) I thought of my father, who was a jet plane pilot.

17) I remembered once, when I was about five, my father returned from a flight in the Philippines and gave me a carved wooden mask he'd bought there, saying, "Son, I just want you to know you're going to die one day. Don't worry about it too much now. But you should know that one day you'll be dead for good and I just want you to be comfortable with that." The night he gave me that mask, and every night since, I've lain awake wondering how soon I'd shuffle off this mortal coil. 18) I tried to envision, exactly, what a mortal coil might look like.

19) With my head on the cold, lumpy pillow I started to think how thoughts are things that happen, how mental activity constitutes an event, how thought is an occurrence that consumes time the same as washing dishes, for example, or building a garage. 20) I felt pleased with the postulation. 21) I saw myself recumbent upon the orange and brown quilt, thinking: a bed-prone idler, philosophical and relaxed.

22) The fly came back, loud as a lawnmower. 23) Not everything is in the mind, I thought. 24) If I had a sawed-off shotgun, I said to myself, I'd take care of his number.

25) Okay, I said, *nap*. 26) I tried to shut my eyes, but realized they were shut. 27) I remembered I'd shut them back when I'd tried to envision what a mortal coil might look like.

28) With deliberation, I began to breathe deeply. 29) In a half-hearted fashion, I started counting sheep. 30) I counted six sheep jumping over the Chrysler building. 31) The sun I envisioned was a dripping amber coin. 32) The sheep wore day-glo togas and sunglasses. 33) People were filing out of the Chrysler building in business suits, eating yogurt with long spoons. 34) My father was there, emerging from foggy dream visualization in a jacket and tie, wearing the Philippine death mask, saying, "Good to see you; son; good to see you're still around." My father told me I'd better do something with my life soon because I was going to die someday. "Start now," he said. "Take my advice."

35) I decided that to follow one's father's advice is suicidal. 36) I decided we all have our own footsteps to follow.

38) Trouble was, I had to admit, I wasn't doing much. Some thinking, sure, which passed the time, but that was the extent of it. 39) I rearranged the pillow beneath my head. 41) I told myself I should be out looking for a job.

40) Just then I heard what sounded like gasps leaking through the apartment wall. 41) When I lifted my head, the mucus rivulet made a break for my upper lip, 42) but I whipped it back with a sharp sniff.

43) The guy who lives next door, Walter, is seventy-five years old and until last week went to work everyday at the garage he opened in the '40s. Every evening for two years I watched him hobble down the hall in his grease-stained coveralls, wrenches and ratchet-clamps rattling his utility belt. When I asked him why he was retiring, he grunted. I thought: Wouldn't it be awful if Walter really *was* dying over there? 44) I thought of him sitting alone, eating his heated up T.V. dinner—pepper steak and peach cobbler—watching reruns of game shows on television. What if he suddenly had a heart attack and is gasping out with no one to help him? I thought. Should I call an ambulance?

45) The fly made a great Dopplering arc past my ass. 46) I remembered how the last girl I'd dated told me how her father, a successful businessman, had died while driving to an out of town convention. He was supposed to be gone for a week, so no one knew anything was wrong until eight days later. "That's terrible," I'd said. "Well," she'd said, "at least he'd done pretty well for himself up to that point." That girl's name was Marjorie.

47) Opening my eyes, I saw on the ceiling a familiar, diffuse crack on the verge of becoming two cracks. 48) I glanced at the clock and noticed it was 2:37. 49) I wondered: Is my clock slow?

50) I remembered meeting Marjorie at the Laundromat while she was waiting for me to finish using the dryer. She helped me find my other sock. I noticed her black hair and glasses. She was skinny, and her chin went straight to her throat, but she folded her clothes so neatly that I was intrigued and asked her on a date, which was a disaster. Over dinner she asked me what I did, and the conversation went downhill from there. "I'm sure you'll do something soon," she said. When we kissed at the end of the night

it made a sound like a cricket. "Will I see you again?" she asked. "Sure," I said. "Soon."

51) I experienced a pang like the bang of a garbage can lid. 52) The thought bubbled and popped in my mind: I am unlucky in love. 53) The Buddhists have not considered certain phenomena, I thought. The monks of Tibet, with their orange robes and bowls of rice, don't have to worry about unemployment, or Freudian-coded phobias of one's father. Life is pushing on and I am going to die one day. Is loneliness only in the mind as well?

54) A quick sniff of the mucoid trickle.

55) The covers scraped stiff and itchy beneath me; the pillow bunched and shapeless as my day. 56) I closed my eyes to conjure sleep, but sleep, the idea and the actuality, was in another century.

57) Suddenly, with a deafening *bzzzzt*, the fly landed on my forehead. 58) Reaching my hand up to brush it away, I accidentally slapped myself in the eye. 59) The fly flew off.

60) My father always told me to take careful notice of flies because they existed, he said, to symbolize decay, to feed on the waste and excrement of our daily living, our garbage cans and piles of filth. That to be aware of them was to be aware of how death is always about us. "Death in the form of the wily black insect," he explained. "Scanning with its prismatic eye to find a death source to steal from, rubbing its crooked forelegs together in the manner of malicious scheming, wondering which refuse to suck up next." Rushing off to work in the morning, adjusting his tie, my father would inevitably shout, "No flies on me!" At the dinner table, to show he was cultured, he would quote that Emily Dickinson poem: "I heard a fly buzz."

61) My eye stung nastily from the accidental slap.

62) I imagined Walter's corpse next door, stiffening at his dinner table for weeks, undiscovered like Marjorie's father in his car, turning colors. The body of Walter, slumped over his peach cobbler, the scotch tape on his Mercedes posters peeling from the wall. 63) I imagined a colony of flies burrowing through the wall, coming into my apartment through the crack in my ceiling. 64) I imagined hordes of flies swarming over the death mask of my father's face, which is also my face. 65) I thought: I am not like him, despite the fact that I look, talk, walk, and act like him.

66) I shifted my weight and the bedsprings eked beneath me like an underworld. 67) The fly *bzzzted* to the windowsill. 68) In the then calming quiet of the room, I heard my stomach rumble. 69) There was a feeling in my belly I could only define as hunger. If Marjorie could see me now, would she feel disgust or pity? A hungry, unemployed man lying on his bed in the middle of the day in what she would call an unclean room? I would deny it—"It's clean," I'd say. "Then why is there a fly in it?" she'd ask. She'd probably say: "How can you lie there dreaming of decay? Don't you see the death mask, hovering over your face, waiting to affix itself?" 70) I could see Marjorie's eyes, studying me through her prismatic glasses.

71) Right there, on the orange and brown quilt, I felt a sudden rush of self-affirmation. 72) I decided I was not myself, despite the fact that I look, talk, walk and act like myself. 73) By not being myself, I am all the more myself!, I thought. Multi-dimensional and free! While one me seems to lie here, the other is solving problems!

74) The realization made me feel immediately better. 75) Realizations are a type of work, I autodidactized. I've been working the whole time I've been lying here. Time has been passing in a productive and positive manner!

76) It occurred to me I was so hungry I could eat the future. 77) I sat up on the bed and blew the rivulet of mucus from my nose into a clean Kleenex. 78) I made mental preparations for going in the kitchen to make myself a cheese sandwich.

79) Just then there was a knock at the door. 80) I imagined for a moment it might be the fly, asking if I would please let him out—a request I would be happy to accommodate. 81) I got off the bed and moved to the door with zest and alacrity. There were no flies on me!

82) When I opened the door I saw the stooped, crusty frame of Walter from next door, wearing his greasy overalls. He wanted to know if he could borrow some sugar. 83) I leapt forward and embraced him warmly. 84) The fly flew into the corridor with a sonic *whoosh*, free at last.

85) "What the hell is your problem?" Walter croaked.

86) "Nothing," I said. "Why?"

Baseball Is Dangerous but Love Is Everything

Upon a time once, wakes up Joe in the sober red morning. Sitting, in shorts, at the edge bed's and a smile of remembered with the events last night. His bad problem despite he had anyway gone out to a bar. A nice dress was there in a woman of distinction who asked why he so strangely spoke and mixed up too? Another Joe ordered drink and a told of the story her he was when little playing a game, baseball, and clobbered an older kid on the head with him a bat. Laughing, laughing the other kids did when saw blood and everyone little Joe's mushed skull. Was on from then Joe's brain a not-right scramble and his thinking irregular slightly.

"That's terrible," the woman said.

Joe thought had he never seen celestial beauty in such a face. "Will to me be you my suckle of honey?" he stammered.

"I'd love to," the woman said.

Parted the clouds and shines the sun in.

"I'm cured," Joe cried, and ran to hold her in his arms.

Really Happy Day

Earlier today, as I was walking through the business district, a slice of pie fell at my feet. I was passing under an awning when it clattered to the pavement—chokecherry pie on a clear glass plate. I gave myself a little hug.

Later, on a different street—or the same street with a different name—I held out my hand to check for rain and a brown beaded handbag landed in my palm. The bag sported an elegant leather strap, and seemed to be made in Morocco. I said, "All right."

I opened the bag, rummaged around in some crinkly tissue, and found a handgun, which I pulled out and fired. The bullet hit a falling persimmon, which exploded, naturally, splattering scarlet fruit all over an ophthalmologist's office, an abstract blast of wet red motion. That made me so happy I could hardly contain myself: I started running home, leaping over construction pylons and rubbing my hands together.

But I hadn't gone two blocks when a uniformed nurse hailed me from her apartment and, almost simultaneously, from atop a double-decker bus, a stranger tossed me a waffle. It was a little late for breakfast, but I was grateful for the nourishment. I also relished the prospect of a soft nurse who knew my name. From where I stood I saw her, disrobing on the fire escape.

This was turning out to be the best day of my life.

In the distance then, about eight blocks away, a clown came wheeling up waving an ossified human bone, as if to say: Nothing is known; why not just enjoy it? His puffy rubber shoes were painted pink and green. The clown approached, lifted his arms high over his head, and passed me a basketball. And then the storm clouds started shaking, and the sky filled up with light.

Lint

Suddenly, there was a great deal of lint. We woke up one day and our coffee cups were filled with it. Out in the car the bucket seats were covered and there was lint on the turn signal, lint in the radio, lint coming out of the slatted air vents. A creepy suspicion slipped into our hearts. Just going to the supermarket was totally impossible now.

"Is this the accumulation of everything rubbed off from us?" someone asked.

"The fuzzy by-product of what's lost and forgotten?" said another.

We looked, but our pasts were obscured from view and a shadow loomed up, plague-like. Winter arrived, and cold sunlight shone through fibrous clouds. Lint blew about like snow, latticing the trees with fine, raveled webs. "Lint!" we yelled at the holidays, amid litters of Christmas paper, "You shouldn't have!"

We were frightened, but deeply intrigued; scientists and psychics were consulted. Philosophers gave symposia, but by then even words themselves were lint: a soft, matted language of purples and blues.

These days it is difficult to blink or lift a finger: we're packed in on every side, struck dumb with wonder. It used to be we moved through life believing everything is understood but the lone, immutable secret that forever eludes our grasp. The lint has reminded us that this is not the case. In truth, we are the fixed point, and it is the secret that reaches out, from every direction, for us.

Found Story

I set out to touch something real. My fingers missed dinner plates, ticket stubs, photographs, and clothes. In the crowd-filled street I grasped the shoulders of strangers, thinking this is what it is to be human.

But my own body got invisible. Passersby cast glances in me while I crisscrossed the earth many times until I found you, on a park bench, reading a storybook.

"Look," I said, with my hand out, "I'm here."

In this story, the you is specifically you, eyes looking up from the page as if a train had just stopped, and the sound of a spiraling bird filled the sky.

"I found this gift," I sighed. "And I so much want you to have it."

Abandoned Belongings

I gave up my childhood dreams as impractical and far-fetched, and became instead a peddler of vegetables. I pushed my cart through the village square in the late afternoons, hawking onions and yams, calling to customers, shop merchants, the children of acquaintances.

One day, during my rounds, I spied the wizened figure of a monk, reading alone in the shade of a baobab tree. As I approached, I saw that his face was the width of a nickel, his eyes were speck-like dashes, and the skin of his hands shone smooth as polished rock. On his back was a little red backpack.

"Sir," I said. "Excuse me for disturbing you, but I can see you are wise in the ways of the soul, and your heart must be very deep indeed. I've always longed to pursue a spiritual life, and would be grateful if you could give me even the simplest kind of advice, some small piece of knowledge to start me on my way, in the right direction, as it were."

The monk peered at me with a puzzled expression. Around us, wind was lifting the day's lazy heat and some birds circled high overhead. I waited what seemed several minutes, but the monk said nothing. Finally his tiny face widened, wrinkles cracking outward, and he inhaled, gathering a loose fold of robe in his fist. Then, like a shot, he sneezed on his sleeve.

The monk removed a tissue from the backpack and wiped his face and clothes. Without a glance in my direction he stood and walked away, a midget-sized man, hunched, but moving quickly. He cut to the edge of the square, then ran past the town's outer houses and disappeared among the whisperweed.

I turned to peruse his abandoned belongings. His monk backpack was filled with nothing but tissue, his monk book was written in a language I didn't know.

A fat leaf swept across the cobblestones, and I felt a strange satisfaction inside, as though all of my mistakes were just precisely right.

Looking around, I noticed the square was deserted, and I was alone with my cart.

Quickly, I ate a potato with my bare hands. Then I knelt down, and washed my face in the public fountain.

Acknowledgments

Portions of this book have appeared in the following publications:

3 AM Magazine: "Accident by Escalator";
Alaska Quarterly Review: "Answering Machine";
Denver Quarterly: "A Primer";
Dirt: "Jane and I at Home One Sunday";
Double Room: "I'd Heard She Had a Deconstructive Personality";
Ducky: "Nothing Bad Happens Here" and "Family Scandal";
elimae: "In Love With Nowhere to Go";
Hayden's Ferry Review: "The Metaphysics of Orange Juice";
In Posse Review: "The Enigma of Possibility" and "The Suicide";
La Petite Zine: "Dan Meets Dave";
Opium: "86 Things That Happened Between 2:35 and 2:38 While I Was Lying on My Bed Trying to Take a Nap," "The Great Grandson of J. Alfred Prufrock" and "The Reason We Were So Afraid";
PP/FF: An Anthology: "Leaving Places" and "Same Game";
Paragraph: "Impressionism";
Pindeldyboz: "True Confessions of the Bat-Fonz" and "The New Duchamp";
Quarterly West: "Allegorical Story with Literal Window";
Quick Fiction: "The Task," "Baseball Is Dangerous but Love Is Everything," "Westminster March," "Woodpecker," and "Really Happy Day";
River City: "Compliments";
Salt Hill: "Getting Older," "Macho Outing," and "The Unfortunate Poker Game";

Sentence: "Invention of the Offenbach";

Spork: "What I'm Doing After This," "Working Out with Kafka" and "Goodbye Now";

Swink: "Eavesdropping at the Van Gogh Museum";

Sudden Stories: A Mammoth Anthology of Miniscule Fiction: "I Carry a Hammer in My Pocket for Occasions Such as These";

Wild Strawberries: "A Telephone Conversation with My Father";

Word Riot: "My Nap."

Much gratitude to the following artists and friends for their support: D. and N. Achs, J. Allen, N. Arnold, J. Ashley, C. Beneke, J. Bowman, D. Cash, J. Chibbaro, P. Conners, N. Danzinger, S. Dougal, S. Dybek, L. Eckle, K. Fitzpatrick, D. Freeling, J. Freeman, R. Giles, M. Goldberg, J. Little, C. Lott, J. Petropoulos, P. Martia, N. Magill, D. Manchester, K. Marzahl, S. McCormick, K. Nash, E. O'Brien, L. Rogers, T. Simmonds, J. Smith, D. Stonecipher, J. Story, J.M. Superville, T.A. Ward, D. Young. Thanks also to Wendy Schmalz. And to my mother and father. And my brother.

This book is dedicated to the spirit that made it and, likewise, to everyone who reads it.

About the Author

Anthony Tognazzini was born in California and has lived in the Philippines, Texas, Spain, Germany, Indiana, and the Czech Republic. He currently lives in New York City.

❖ ❖ ❖

BOA Editions, Ltd.
American Reader Series

❖ ❖ ❖

Colophon

I Carry A Hammer In My Pocket For Occasions Such As These, stories by Anthony Tognazzini, was designed by Richard Foerster, York Beach, Maine, and is set in ITC Veljovic, a font designed by Jovica Veljovic (1954–) that displays a crisp precision, as if the letters were cut in stone rather than drawn with pen and ink. The cover design is by Steve Smock of Prime 8 Media. The cover art is by Erica Harris. Manufacturing is by McNaughton & Gunn, Saline, Michigan.

The publication of this book is made possible, in part, by the special support of the following individuals:

Anonymous (5)
Susan DeWitt Davie
Peter & Sue Durant
Kip & Deb Hale
Robin & Peter Hursh
Archie & Pat Kutz
Craig & Susan Larson
Stanley D. McKenzie
Boo Poulin
Roland Ricker
TCA Foundation on behalf of Mid-Town Athletic Club
Philip Timpane
Ellen Wallack
Lee & Rob Ward
Thomas R. Ward, in memory of Jane Buell Ward
Mike & Pat Wilder
Glenn & Helen William